RELEASER

Stefanie Dawn

Releaser
Elements of Abduction
Book 5

Stefanie Dawn

This book is a work of fiction. Any references to real events, real people, and real places are used fictitiously. Other names, characters, places and incidents are products of the Author's imagination and any resemblance to persons, living or dead, actual events, organizations or places is entirely coincidental.

All rights are reserved. This book is intended for the purchaser of this book ONLY. No part of this book may be reproduced or transmitted in any form or by any means, graphic, electronic, or mechanical, including photocopying, recording, taping, or by any information storage retrieval system, without the express written permission of the Author. All songs, song titles and lyrics contained in this book are the property of the respective songwriters and copyright holders.

Disclaimer: The material in this book contains graphic language and sexual content and is intended for mature audiences, ages 18 and older.

ISBN: 978-1763870529
Editing and Proofing by Swish Design & Editing
Book Design by Swish Design & Editing
Cover Design by Eric at
The Book Brander
Published by Angels and Fire Books
Cover Image Copyright 2024

DEDICATION

To all my alien peen queens.

RELEASER

CHAPTER I

AMY

Rancid fruit.

That's what they smelled like—the scent where fruit begins to turn and is almost fermenting, and you'd pull back from the refrigerator thinking, *God, how long have* those *been in there?* Some remnant from an attempt to change my diet.

I could forgive myself for having incoherent thoughts as I was pulled from a pod in a lab of some sort.

By *aliens.*

There was no way I could look around the room fast enough, and nothing seemed to be registering in my mind. Every time I blinked, it was a harsh squeeze shut of my eyes, hoping they would clear, or even better—that the things I *thought* I was seeing would disappear. Everything was strange, instruments and beings that made no sense, and each visual only increased the panic in my chest. Each thump of my heart was a warning I was in danger, but my vision shifted in and out of focus as I tried to take everything in.

Where was I?

How did I get here?

Blinking through the confusion, images flashed across my mind as I struggled to piece together the information as I was dragged onto a table. I wanted to fight off the aliens, but my limbs ached like nothing I'd ever experienced before. Not necessarily the worst pain I'd ever had, but a bone-deep ache that made lifting any limb nearly impossible. It was like gravity was stronger, and simply shifting a finger was more effort than I could manage. My head throbbed, and my stomach churned as if I were going to be sick. The feeling would pass, only to come back again, stronger in the next wave of nausea. Groaning, I rolled my head to the side on the cold table. The aliens moved around me, and they passed things to each other while they chatted in their bizarre language.

Were they *really* aliens?

Yes.

I knew they were. I was certain of it.

There wasn't a hint of doubt in my mind—*and why was that?*

Surely, my first thought should have been that maybe I was imagining things or simply dreaming. Perhaps any sane person would have tried to convince themselves these beings were humans in weird costumes.

But there was no bargaining in my mind to replace reality with some story I made up. I had accepted they were aliens as quickly as I had blinked when I was released from the pod. The knowledge came to me with absolute clarity that not only were these aliens, but I was on an alien planet.

But how did I know these things?

Think, Amy. Think!

The grogginess was difficult to clear, and my sight kept washing out with spotted grays and bright lights that faded from the edges of my vision.

Think!

What happened?

I'd been home, and then…

Oh my God. I was *abducted.*

But not by these aliens, by different ones, who were shorter and rounder, with long arms that seemed disproportionate to their bodies. Two arms or four? I couldn't remember. Perhaps I'd only seen a shadow of them, or they moved very quickly. But I was taken with five other girls.

My throat ached as I gasped loudly, the memory of the other girls coming back to me.

Deborah, Tegan, Monica, Luna, and Rebecca.

Where are they?

I cried out as a needle was thrust into my arm, and with the searing pain came a rush of memories that made my head spin. My eyes were wide open as I stared at the bright light in the ceiling above me. I remembered. We'd been delivered directly from the other aliens to these ones—the Ghaal. The aliens who had abducted us landed their ship in the middle of the Ghaal's village, and we were shoved into their arms, their mouths twisted in dark smirks as they snarled at us in their language.

There were experiments I don't remember the details of, and maybe that was for the best.

We lived in a cell together, and one by one, the girls were taken and didn't come back. Until there was only Tegan and me left, and when they came for us, we were certain we were going to die. There was screaming and panic, and I couldn't be certain if it was us screaming or the Ghaal. But the wall opened with a hiss, and we were shoved into pods.

And that's the last thing I remembered until now.

One of the Ghaal snapped his fingers in front of my face. "Female. Pay attention."

Hatred mingled with the fear that flowed freely through my system, and I narrowed my eyes as I glared at the male alien. He accepted my eye contact as confirmation that I was listening to him, and a pinpoint light was shone into my eyes. I recoiled from it only to have my chin grabbed and the light flashed across my eyes again.

"Pupils normal. Heart rate normal. Muscles recovering. You've emerged from stasis in good condition."

Stasis?

"You froze me?" I cleared my throat. It hurt to talk.

"We preserved you until more females could be found to replace the ones destroyed in the experiments."

My arm twitched even through the weight of my fatigue as I went to grip my chest. "De—*destroyed?*"

Of course, Tegan and I had assumed the worst when it came to the fate of the other girls, but to have it confirmed in such a clinical manner exploded snakes in my stomach until I was fighting back the urge to dry retch.

"They didn't survive the tests. But we found out what we needed to know."

"Oh God..." Tears blurred my vision, and I wanted to swipe them away, but all I could manage was another lurch of my arm, and my shoulder jerked as I tried to lift the limb.

Dead.

All of them dead.

I'd been particularly close to Rebecca as we had

shared the same quiet personality and gravitated toward each other. She was the last to be taken by the Ghaal from our shared cell.

"Please, please take me instead," I begged and tried to hide Rebecca behind me. I was taller and bigger than her, but that was useless when it came to facing the full height and force of these aliens. Of course, I knew that. I couldn't get that fact out of my head, but that didn't stop me from trying. They'd taken everyone else, and we'd fought every time. I'd fight again for Rebecca. They couldn't have her.

When the Ghaal reached into the cell with their horrible cattle-prod weapons at the ready and tried to grab Becca, I lost whatever semblance of control I had left. I wasn't the strongest person at the best of times, but my connection to her made me want to fight. She was all I had left. Becca reminded me of my niece, Trudy—the daughter of my eldest sister, a fourteen-year gap between my sister and me—and I'm sure my niece would have grown up to be like Becca—sweet, kind, and quiet like me. Trudy and I would've bonded over that as she got older. I was certain of it.

If I were still on Earth and had the chance.

If my life hadn't been taken away from me.

Becca was my family now. They couldn't take her.

"Stand aside."

I was surprised the Ghaal bothered to talk to me at all. Usually, they simply shoved us to the side and took who they wanted, ignoring our futile attempts to attack them. But with each girl who was taken, the Ghaal's physical contact with us became less frequent and violent, almost as if they were afraid to hurt us. I couldn't decipher their behavior, and any attempts to communicate with them to find out what was going on were met with disinterested silence.

"You are the youngest." The statement was directed toward Becca, but I shifted my body again to hide her further and kept her behind my back with a wave of my hand.

"What does that matter?" I snapped, feeling none of the bravery my voice portrayed.

The Ghaal's eyes landed on mine, the orange ring to the irises blazing a hole through me and rooting me to the spot. They'd told us all about their history when we were first delivered to them, how they were almost wiped out and needed virile females to breed, and how it was a great honor for us to be here.

How it would be easier if we cooperated.

Monica had been the first to be taken by them. She'd been almost catatonic from the moment we landed, and she continued to show no emotion as she was led away.

We never saw her again.

And now they wanted Becca because she was the youngest. Why?

Something passed across the Ghaal's eyes. Could it have been sympathy? Impossible, considering our situation and how they treated us.

"Her body is virile. She will do the best with the tests."

Becca squealed from behind me before the sound dissolved into a sob. We had no idea what was done to the girls once they were taken from the cell, but given the Ghaal were all about using us to breed, our imaginations ran wild.

Tests she needed to be young and virile for?

"Absolutely fucking not. You leave her alone." I held my ground and tried to hide the trembling of my hands.

The Ghaal raised his weapon as the two behind him chuckled, all of them ignoring Tegan as she cowered in the corner behind us all and sobbed quietly. "Stand aside, female, or you will be forced to."

"No, no!" I cried out. I leaped at them as they moved around me, but they shoved me to the side as if I was nothing more than a mere inconvenience and grabbed Becca's arm. The edge of the weapon hit my lower back as I moved at them again. I screamed and crumpled to the floor before I reached up and held a hand out as Becca

was led from the cell.

"Becca!"

"Amy!" Her blonde hair was in knots as it fell down her back, and the dirt on her face from weeks in captivity was streaked with tears. As soon as I could move after the shock of the prod had subsided and the twitching of my muscles eased, I ran on shaking legs to the bars and ignored the biting cold as I wrapped my fingers around them. I shook and tried to rattle the bars as the door at the end of the hallway was closed, and Becca disappeared from sight.

The same as the others.

Never to come back.

"Bring her back!" I screamed, crying openly now. "Please, bring her back."

The Ghaal who'd stayed behind as Becca was taken pinched my chin between his fingers and tilted my face to his. "Stay calm, female. You'll have your turn soon."

She was gone.

Becca was gone.

I'd been yanked away from my family on Earth, and now the family I had here was taken from me too. Tegan and I had been close only through circumstance, but we were two people who would have never interacted back on Earth. She was a cheerleader, literally—in high school, college, and now professionally. And what was I? Always picked last for sports, I wouldn't have even *dreamed* of attending cheerleading tryouts. Three sizes too big for them to even look at me twice. I could dance, though, but only with my sisters in our rooms.

I was a mathematics nerd who realized very quickly that, out of college, finding a job to fit my qualifications wasn't easy. While I wasn't even certain of what career path I wanted to take, I was never given a chance to pursue anything.

But all of that was gone. Everything I knew, everyone I loved, and everything I had hoped or dreamed of achieving had been swiped away from me because these fuckers decided they wanted to use us for our wombs.

"How long?" I managed to croak out, swallowing and immediately regretting it when the only result was a sharp sting.

"What?" the Ghaal snapped, placing another instrument down on a table after poking it against my neck.

"How long was I frozen?"

"You weren't *frozen,* you were in stasis—"

I cleared my throat enough to snap back at him, "I don't give a shit about semantics. *How long?*"

His eyes flashed at my tone, but he took no disciplinary action. "Approximately twelve cycles of the sun."

"Twelve *years?*"

He waved his hand. "I do not know what it translates to on your planet, and I don't care. Now get up. You need to go back to your cell."

The table I lay on started to tilt, and pins and needles shot from my toes to my hips as my feet hit the floor, and I struggled to stand. My nudity was brought to my full attention as the leers of the alien men around me needled into my skin, and I covered myself with shaking hands. A simple tunic was thrust in my direction, and I hurried to put it on. It barely came to my thighs, but it was better than nothing.

The walk back to the same cell I'd been in before—*years* before—was a short one. Exit the lab, into a hall, one turn, another door, another short hall, and there was the cell. The length of the hall with the bars running from one wall to another, the remaining three sides of the cell were a cold stone or metal, I could never figure out what. My chest ached when I realized how pathetically short the walk from the lab had been, yet it was one Becca and the other girls only ever made in one direction.

Was I the lucky one to still be alive?

I wasn't sure.

As I was shoved into the cell, Tegan pushed herself up from where she had been crouched in the corner, and the ache in my chest throbbed at the sight of her. I wanted to celebrate she was alive, but that response was instantly deflated by the harsh reality of what awaited us here.

"Amy," she whispered and brought me into an awkward hug. I lifted one arm and patted her on the back. There was nothing warm about our reunion. Perhaps instead of a touch or *Thank God, you're alive,* it was mostly, *Thank God, I'm not alone in this hell.*

As I flinched when the cell door was closed behind me, I realized I couldn't blame Tegan if that's how she felt about me. Nothing more than the comfort of comradery and someone familiar. Because that's how I felt too.

Thank God I'm not alone.

But those thoughts came with a sting of guilt, for it meant Tegan was in for the same hell as I was.

We sunk to the floor against the rear wall, so close our arms brushed together, and we said nothing.

What is there to say?

We knew what fate awaited us.

CHAPTER
2

ELDICH

The Moeks were rarely so poor with their aim of the units that they landed near my home, and I suspected even fewer would have landed near Ryth. They wanted to get them as close to the Ghaal colony as possible since that's where they would collect their bounty.

But my brothers and I still needed to cover as much ground as we could, making sure any species abducted from other planets and left here knew to stay away from the Ghaal colony. The Ghaal—so desperate to rebuild their numbers after almost wiping themselves out—had resorted to kidnapping other species to find a genetic match capable of breeding with. They would impregnate a compatible species by any means necessary, including surgery, no matter how torturous it would be for the victims who fell into their hands.

Over the years, several species had been abducted and dropped here. My brothers and I were across this area of the continent and did our best to ensure any displaced species didn't fall into the hands of the Ghaal. We would communicate with them if we could and attempt to direct them to safety. There was no way for them to go home, so they needed to do the best they could with their new life here. This was a bountiful planet, capable of being home to many lifeforms. It had replenished after the Ghaal wars, produced numerous foods, and sustained the remaining animal life enough that their numbers could flourish.

The woodlands I called home were a few days' journey from my nearest brothers. Ryth resided where the river systems took over before they stretched into large lakes in a dense rainforest smattered with crisscrossing waterways. Lanir lived in the ashy mountains closer to the Ghaal colony. I had volunteered to go out the farthest, being quite content with being alone. But Ryth had taken that post, insisting it was as important as being the nearest, and he was strong enough to handle the isolation.

I didn't doubt he was strong enough, but I wondered about his motivations. Even in captivity, he seemed intent on going above and beyond to prove himself as strong as the rest of us—a streak of pride that drove most of his actions.

But while content with being alone, it had been many years since I'd lived in the company of my brothers, and I missed them. This was the life we chose, to do what we could to save beings from falling victim to the Ghaal. Synths were not violent if we could avoid it, and the Ghaal had the one thing that could kill us instantly if we tried to interfere.

How much good could we do if we were dead?

In the Ghaal's hands, we were tools, and if we became a nuisance, we were to be put down.

So, it's better we work from a distance.

My foot wedged between two branches. Flimsy to an onlooker, these trees were surprisingly strong, equally as flexible, and excellent for creating traps to lure prey for food. From atop the tree, I had seen more units drop. The tiny shapes fell to the planet's surface and landed nearer to the colony than I resided. Once again, I wouldn't be needed, but I didn't resent that.

I was here if I were ever needed to help.

I counted four units as they dropped and frowned.

The Ghaal always worked in sixes. *Always.* I had five brothers, making six Synths in total, and every other unit drop had been six. It was more than a superstition. It dated back to the Ghaal's ancient religions and rituals before the wars. Their belief was it was the abandonment of their commitment to six and all its sacred meaning that led to the wars and, ultimately, their demise in the first place. So, generations ago, the survivors gathered themselves and vowed to uphold the beliefs this time.

So why only four units?

With the units' wing mechanism activated, they safely drifted toward the surface. I lost track of three of them over the mountains, but the fourth came down on this side in Lanir's territory.

He would find the being inside and ensure they were safe.

A couple of weeks passed, give or take, and I gave the units no further thought. They weren't in my territory, and therefore, there was no sense in traveling to them.

The last thing I expected to see within my woodland home's dominant yellow and white colors was Lanir.

I knew it was him from how he moved and held himself, as though with every step he was heading into battle, the entire world an enemy force. Synths were designed to adapt to our environments, which is why my skin was the same color as the sandy soil, streaked with white so I could blend in with the trees and foliage. It was why my fingers and toes were longer than they used to be, to make climbing and gripping easier. However, Lanir's skin was a deep, ashy gray, almost black, streaked with red cracks as though he were made of the rocks of his mountain home.

I didn't bother hiding myself and stayed where I perched atop a tall tree, knowing if he looked up, he'd be able to see me over the treetops. Even from the distance, our eyes locked—our eyes bright green, the only thing we still had in common with our appearances. I couldn't read his expression, but then again, this was Lanir, and he was closed off to the world, including the only family he had. There was no way to know what he was thinking unless he *wanted* you to know.

I understood him. We'd been through torture as brothers, and even when we banded together after we escaped from the Ghaal, I kept to the precipice of our circle. I kept my distance lest I again became weak around them. Lanir had the same fear, though he would never express it, and stalked around the edge of the camp if he ever stayed near us. But mostly, he kept to himself and fled to live in solidarity at the earliest chance he had.

Lanir stopped under the tree I stood in, and I slowly descended.

"They're compatible," Lanir grunted when my feet hit the sandy soil.

"The females in the latest unit drop?" Lanir

wasn't much one for greetings or talking, and I worked to put things together from the few words he offered. Once his words hit me, I struggled to keep myself concentrating when a million questions ran through my mind. I wanted *all* the information about the females. I wanted everything he could give me, but Lanir would drip-feed me snippets unless I asked leading questions and pushed him hard.

The Ghaal had found compatible females.

So why was Lanir here to tell me?

And why Lanir specifically? I would have expected Ilk, Sahcor, or someone of a more level head.

Had something happened to them?

No, don't get ahead of yourself.

Lanir's brows drew together as these thoughts raced through my mind, and my patience grew thin. "Whatever your adversity to talking, Lanir, you're here for a reason. Tell me the entire story from start to finish and what you need of me." My voice held no aggression or challenge, but Lanir still bristled at my words. I was thankful to see one of my brothers after all these years, but the circumstances were strange. "Talk," I repeated when he didn't immediately offer an explanation.

"Four units dropped, containing human females from a planet called Earth. They are compatible with the Ghaal, and we have rescued them."

I assumed *we* meant Ilk, Sahcor, Vitri, and Lanir,

given the units dropped on that side of the mountains. I said nothing and waited.

"But these are not the first humans the Ghaal had taken. Given the evidence we saw, Ilk and I assumed the last lot was killed with the experiments. It turns out two of the human females are still in Ghaal captivity. We intend to save them."

My eyes widened as it came together. There *were* six females, and the four most recent drops were to bring the numbers back to six.

Six females compatible for mating and breeding, and six of us.

My eyes glazed over as my instinct to breed reared its head, and I tried to maintain concentration.

I was brought crashing back to the moment by Lanir's snarl. "Now is not the time to be thinking of mating." Lanir would have known immediately where my thoughts drifted, but I couldn't help it. My desire to breed was as much a part of my DNA as it was his. Simply because Lanir had longer to get used to the information of compatible females didn't mean he had the right to be aggressive toward me for responding with instinct.

However, he was right. This wasn't the time, but I still growled at his words. "You need me and Ryth back to help save the other females?"

"Yes. You are to go to Ryth. We will explain more when you get back to Ilk's."

"Why do you not continue on to get Ryth yourself?" Again, I delivered my words with no anger. It was simply a question of curiosity, but Lanir took it as a challenge and growled in response.

He pulled himself to his full height, his chest out, and a glint of pride in his expression I'd never seen from him before. "My mate waits for me at Ilk's. I will get back to her."

My shoulders tensed. "Your mate?"

"One of the human females."

The constriction in my chest was replaced by a hollow ache and a thudding of my heart, which I'm certain Lanir could hear. One of the females had already been claimed. There were only five left. I had to hope one of them liked me.

Outside of my control, my pheromones pumped from my pores—designed to entice a female to me—and this time, Lanir let loose a roar. "This is *not the time.*"

"I'm not doing it on purpose," I snarled back. He had *claimed* his mate. Surely, he knew my immediate response would be to consider the possibility of claiming one of the females as my own.

I'd been alone for so long I wondered how easy they were to talk to.

Do they laugh? Will they tell me about their planet?

I wondered what they looked like.

Would they like me?

"Go to Ryth's. Bring him back to Ilk's."

After a prolonged stare between us, Lanir turned and left without another word.

There was no point in hesitating. I could collect food and water along the way, so I spun on my heel and launched into a full run toward Ryth's territory. I didn't know exactly where he resided in the river system, but he would be easy enough to find.

And if I made enough noise and motion in the water, I knew he'd find me.

CHAPTER
3

AMY

What were they waiting for?

The Ghaal had woken Tegan and me from stasis and moved us back into our cell. It was the same routine as before—food and water delivered twice a day and a small pot in the corner to relieve ourselves. Otherwise, we were left alone. The only difference was this time, we weren't being taken one by one for God knows what experiments and never coming back.

At night, the cell was unbearably cold, and we cuddled up together in a rear corner. There was a barred window, and it offered no protection from the insane winds that came every night, creating strong, icy-cold air that whipped around the cell. If it was this bad inside, I couldn't imagine being outside during the night. Even when I dreamed of escaping, I would find myself in my dream, standing in the middle of a dense forest, with the wind whipping the branches around that would cut and slice into my legs and arms. I wanted to call for help, but I'd be too scared to let the Ghaal know where I was.

Even my dreams of escape were really nightmares.

Tegan and I already knew which corner would offer us the best protection from the chill, and we fell into our old routine as if no time had passed. Because for us, it hadn't felt like years or even days but simply hours. Once our memories returned in full, we may as well not have been frozen in time at all.

There was no point in asking each other questions neither of us had any way of knowing the answers, and our rapid-fire questions to the Ghaal who came in and dropped our food off were ignored.

But we didn't have to wait long for something to change.

"You have what you want. Now, get this fucking thing out of me!"

The voice was unfamiliar but unmistakably

female and *human*. Tegan and I stood and shared a glance before we backed against the cell's rear wall. We'd found this was the move least likely to raise any violence from the Ghaal, and we tucked our hands behind our backs and against the cold wall.

Another human?

"This is why they woke us," I muttered.

"What?" Tegan hissed through her teeth, not taking her eyes off the door at the end of the hall.

"They've abducted more girls and are building the group back up again."

Tegan's teeth started to chatter as fear took hold before the muscles in her jaw tightened as she clenched it. I reached out, took her hand, and gently squeezed her fingers. Tegan's eyes met mine, and she pressed her lips together in a thin imitation of a smile—a silent *thank you* when she couldn't find the words.

The screaming of anger rather than fear had increased now as the door slid open, and two Ghaal entered, dragging a woman between them. She was tall with dark curly hair, and her clothes were strange—they seemed to be made of dark rubber strips woven together. As she got closer, I realized it was seaweed, and my brows drew together as I watched her being pulled toward the cell.

Had she been outside the Ghaal village? Had she escaped somehow?

Could she do it again?

None of us had been able to escape last time. There was simply no chance to. We were delivered directly into the hands of the Ghaal from the aliens who took us. Then we were in this cell, and that was it.

The woman's eyes met ours, immediately filled with sympathy, and I swear she muttered, "Three," under her breath.

But that only raised more questions.

Tegan and I stepped to the side as she was thrown into the cell. She wasted no time in finding her footing, rushed toward the bars to grab them, and shook them as if it would make a difference.

"Get this fucking thing out of my arm. You have what you want," she hissed out the words, and my eyebrows shot up at how bold she was when talking to the Ghaal. Did she not know their cruelty? Their history?

In answer to her attitude, she was poked with the cattle prod-like weapon and screamed as her knees buckled.

My jaw dropped as the Ghaal actually spoke back to her. They had not responded to us in any way since my initial questions after we'd been woken. "In due time, female. We may have been too late to get to the other humans, but we know one thing..." he crouched until his head was level with hers, and her shoulders shook as she met his eyes. "They'll come for you... won't they?"

He left, laughing, and the woman leaned forward, her palms flat on the floor as her shoulders shook slightly. *Is she crying?* Most likely. I squeezed Tegan's hand before letting it go and moved tentatively toward the stranger.

"Are you okay?" My words drew no response from her, but when I touched her shoulder, she jolted before she pushed herself to her feet. I backed away as she grabbed my arms and rubbed her hands up and down them before she cupped my cheeks in her palms.

"Are you okay? Have they touched you? How do you feel? Do you know where you are?"

I opened and closed my mouth a few times before I could process her questions, desperately and rapidly asked one after the other.

Finally, I said, "Who are you?"

Her lips twisted into a grimace, and she dropped her hands from me before she stepped back. She looked at Tegan and me, and her eyes filled with sympathy again before it was quickly replaced by anger.

"Misha, my name is Misha, and I'm a fucking idiot." Before I could respond, she stepped closer to us again, leaned toward me, and hovered her lips near my ear as she whispered, "But don't worry… they'll come save us."

"Who?" I whispered back.

Misha glanced around the cell. "How about we

sit? I feel we have a lot to tell each other."

I nodded, and after a hesitant pause, Tegan followed suit as we sat cross-legged as close as we could get to each other while still maintaining eye contact.

"When did they wake you up?" Misha asked.

"How did you kno—"

Misha held up a hand. "Okay, my story first. It'll be quicker than back-and-forth questions." At my expression, hers softened. "I'm sorry, I'm carrying a lot of anger right now." She sighed and shook her hands out before she squeezed her eyes shut for a moment. "Okay, here we go. Me and three other women were taken from Earth by the Moeks and brought here. We were pushed into little pods and floated to the surface of the planet." Her eyes met mine. "I suspect you were handed directly to the Ghaal from your captors, correct?"

"Yes, but how—"

Misha grabbed one of my hands and one of Tegan's and squeezed. "Please. I have a lot to tell you, and the quicker we're all on the same page, the better. Let me tell you what I know, then you tell me what you know, and we'll go from there, okay?" I nodded as Misha released her hold on my fingers and dragged a hand through her hair. The light from the sun hit it and displayed shades of brilliant red within the dark curls. "I think Sahcor and I had this mostly figured out. So, sometime after you were taken, the planet was cut off from intergalactic trade because of what they did to the other four women you came with. However, the Ghaal wanted more humans because we're compatible with them for breeding, and they want to save their species."

She paused for a moment to glance between Tegan and me. "I can see this part isn't a shock to you. Good. I'd hate to be the bearer of such bad news and figured it was better to rip off the metaphorical Band-Aid." She was still talking quickly, almost jittery, as if desperate to get all the information out as fast as possible. "So, they hired the Moeks… essentially space pirates who would abduct species in exchange for resources and fuel. But it took *years* for them to get more humans." Her stare was serious as she glanced between us. "You've been asleep for a long time."

"A decade at least," I whispered, really only guessing because who knew the relative time difference between this planet and ours? Tegan gasped.

"We have two things working in our favor. One, the Ghaal are superstitious and will only work in sixes, which is why only four of us were taken, because they already had you two. Until they have all the humans together, we're relatively safe." Her lip twisted again as if she wasn't sure about this information and was more *hoping* it was true. "The second thing is the Synths, a species the Ghaal created before they started abducting. They were created for breeding, but the Synths didn't want to help a cruel species, see? So, they escaped, but they're still around. Six of them, big, strong, fast, and determined as hell." Misha lowered her voice even more, and Tegan and I had to lean in to hear her. "They know we're here, and they'll come for us."

There wasn't a flicker of doubt in her face as she said those words.

"Where have you been?" Tegan asked, taking in Misha's odd attire.

Misha's lip twitched into a small smile. "I was rescued by a Synth named Sahcor, and we've been living on a small peninsula. Through a series of fucked-up events, I ended up with a tracker in my arm. We tried to get it out but couldn't. It went off when I came too close to one of the other girls, so I sent her away."

"You've been sleeping with an alien?" Tegan visibly recoiled, and I smirked.

They couldn't all be bad, right? E.T. was friendly. I barely contained my giggle at the idea, and even more so at the way Tegan had *immediately* jumped to them sleeping together.

"Who said anything about *sleeping* with an alien?" I smiled, trying to lighten the mood. Misha had only said she'd been living with him. It made me chuckle that Tegan's mind went straight to sex. But when Misha didn't respond, I turned my gaze slowly toward her, only to find a sheepish grin on her face. "You can't be serious?"

Misha looked as if she was fighting between laughing and remaining impassive. "He's really sweet." It was all she offered, and my jaw dropped.

"You *fucked* an alien?" I hissed, half laughing, half disbelieving.

Misha held up her hands and shushed me. "That's not important right now."

"If you were out there living your best life with a fuckable alien, how did you end up here again?"

Misha huffed out an angry sigh. "I told you because I'm a fucking idiot. Since we couldn't remove the alien tech from my arm, Sahcor and I decided to wait it out and see if they were tracking *me* or if the tracker only went off in the presence of other humans." She glanced at her arm now, and I noted the lump of something under her skin, obscured mostly by a large scar where I assumed she'd tried to dig it out. I shuddered, trying not to think about how much that would have hurt. "Guess they turned it off or some shit," she muttered, rolling her eyes. "Anyway, we waited and set traps to see if the Ghaal would find us. Either they're smarter than I gave them credit for, or I'm stupider." Her face contorted into anger, and then the sneer dropped to concern. "They knew where we were and were just waiting *us* out. We were lured into a false sense of security, and no matter how cautious we were, they were there. We were grabbed, and Sahcor was threatened. I let myself be taken to save him."

"You *let* it happen?"

Misha's eyes filled with tears, and given the way she'd taken command since she set foot in our cell, the effect was disconcerting. "It was the only way to save Sahcor. They were going to kill him." She shook her head as if to shake the emotions away. "But I told you, he'll come for me, for *us*. They all will."

"Who is *all?*"

"The Synths." Misha smiled. "And the Ghaal won't know what hit them."

CHAPTER

4

ELDICH

Being around Ryth after so long should have been a happy moment. The prospect of having females we could make a life with should have only increased the elation. But the thoughts of mating had infected my mind, and Lanir's words rang loudly in my memory. It was all I could think about until my instincts started to come to the surface, and by the time I reached Ryth, I was less myself and more animal than I would've liked.

I hastily explained why I had come for him over the rumble of a growl I couldn't help. My skin felt clammy, and without knowing what the females looked like, somehow my mind conjured images of a mate I could lay underneath me and claim, piercing her with my cock.

My mate waits for me.

Ryth nodded curtly after my explanation, and we were on our way.

What Synths were designed and created for, and all I ever wanted with my mind, body, and soul was a mate. When we were together in captivity in the Ghaal's lab, our mere proximity to each other was enticing us to mate. As a species, we could adapt, and with being so close to each other for extended periods, our desire to mate would take over, and one or more of us would become female.

Will the human females change this about us?

If we have them to mate, could we stay as we are, and my brothers and I can live together again?

Will the females even want me?

So many unanswered thoughts wracked my mind as I looked at my hands while I jogged next to Ryth and studied my elongated fingers. They made climbing trees and crafting with the flexible wood easy. But would I be hideous to the human females? Would they prefer the shorter, sturdier fingers and hands of my brothers? I didn't know what they looked like, but it hardly mattered. Lanir had claimed his mate. Perhaps some of my other brothers had, too, so there must be a level of mutual attraction there.

Ryth stared straight ahead as he ran, most likely lost in his thoughts as I was. A glance down told me he was facing the same problem as I, as his cock was erect as he moved. I was hard, too, and I found my body released my pheromones at the mere *thought* of mating. The pheromones were designed not to drug but simply to increase arousal and put us and our mates in a frenzy of desire.

Resisting the urge to mate had almost killed me when we'd been in captivity. Lanir had begun changing, and the scent of his new female hormones almost drove me to the edge. I still remembered the feeling of my blunt claws cutting into my palms as I tried to resist the change myself when my body started shifting, and I watched the chaos as my brothers fought each other. We were all desperate to keep control but doomed not to have it.

I'd have to get better control of myself before we reached Ilk's and attempted to rescue the remaining females from the Ghaal.

A female wouldn't want a weak male, and I wouldn't want to scare them by becoming no more than an animal in their presence.

Ryth and I kept moving through the night and stopped only for water and food. We pushed ourselves to our limits to get to Ilk's as soon as possible.

As we came over the edge of the mountains, we slowed our pace, and the scent of the females that wafted past on the wind almost had my knees buckling. We found them sitting in a circle. There were three of them, and they sat close enough that they barely had to raise their voices to talk. All I could hear was a muffled whispering in a strange language. One of them turned, and her dark hair, which she wore in a long braid, fell over her shoulder as she gasped and stood before she backed away from Ryth and me. Another stood with her, with lighter hair that shone in the sunlight, and grabbed the arm of the first girl.

She said something to the dark-haired girl with the braid, and her shoulders relaxed.

As the third stood—a taller female with dark hair cropped short—approached us, her smile wide and beautiful. She waved a hand at me, and I glanced at Ryth, unsure what to make of the gesture, as she rattled off a series of strange syllables. When we remained silent, she laughed and turned back to her friends, speaking to them again.

When she faced me, she took another step forward. She barely came up to my chest and looked up at me with a wide grin before she tapped her head, then indicated mine, speaking in that odd language.

"I think she wants you to learn their language," Ryth grunted out.

Of course, she did. I don't know why I didn't think of it. Perhaps because all thoughts had been pushed from my mind at their scents. The females' bodies were small, and each displayed a different shape of curves and natural lines. The light-haired one had wide hips and thighs but a small waist and bust, and I breathed in deeply to get a better scent of her.

And recoiled.

Lanir. His scent was all over her.

This was the one he had claimed as his mate.

Her brows drew together when I had recoiled from her. She repeated the gesture and touched her head before she pointed to mine. Before I could speak, the thundering of footsteps interrupted me. Lanir came from the female's side, scooped her up in his arms, and spun so she was shielded from me by his body. Deep growls rumbled through his chest as she squealed, grabbed his arms, and started talking to him. I growled in return. The female seemed distressed, and perhaps he was frightening her. Lanir snarled at me over his shoulder.

I bared my teeth at him and spread my arms wide, ready to fight.

"Enough!"

We all turned as Ilk approached, Vitri close behind him. I knew it was them mostly from their facial features, but their bodies were so vastly different from how I remembered them. Their appearances made sense—Ilk lived in the mountains, Vitri in the forest—it didn't take much to put together who was who.

I knew we would adapt, but I wasn't prepared for how different we would be from each other when we came back together.

Lanir took a few hurried steps away from Ryth and me, still holding his female. She had slung her arms around his neck and was whispering in his ear, a soothing feminine voice in a language I couldn't yet understand.

She cared for him.

My cock twitched at the thought there would be a female here who would care for me the way I would her. A female with wide hips and thighs, perfect for childbearing. Thighs I could bury my face between and lap at her cunt until her scent was all I knew.

"Ryth. Eldich." Ilk approached us, his lips in a grim line. These were not the ideal circumstances for a reunion, but part of me felt it was overdue. We had been passive in our desire for peace for too long. When the drops became further apart, I had hoped the Ghaal's opportunities had been cut off. But desperation and a lack of a conscience made for a powerful enemy.

I was glad we were going to end this, although I wasn't sure how yet. We were stronger than them, but they could overcome us with numbers.

"I've missed you, brother," I said. Ryth glanced at me as though I'd spoken something strange. But surely, we all missed each other? We were alone in our duty, and I knew I wasn't the only one to feel it.

"We missed you, too," Vitri chimed in, cooing as though talking to a child. I sneered, unable to hold the expression, when he started laughing and I joined in his joy. Ilk smirked as Vitri slapped me on the shoulder. "We better get you up to date with the human language before we do much else."

This elicited another growl from Lanir, audible from where he hovered at the outskirts of our circle, and guilt wracked my system. I hadn't intended to cause a rift so soon, and by reacting to his mate with arousal, I had offended him.

"Lanir," I grunted out, hoping he would look me in the eye, but instead, when he turned, his gaze bounced around the area as if he was fighting the urge to flee. "I didn't know. It won't happen again."

He snorted a huff of air through his nose and nodded stiffly before walking away, still holding his mate tight against his chest. She offered me an apologetic smile, no doubt able to guess the situation even when she couldn't understand our language.

Vitri chuckled, then waved over the other two females. I clenched my fists, willing myself not to respond. The short-haired one went immediately to Vitri's side and the other to Ilk's.

All three females were claimed.

My chest was heavy, and I tried to contain my disappointment. I reminded myself there were still females held by the Ghaal.

My chances weren't entirely lost.

Vitri touched the top of his mate's head. "Tori," he said, then indicated the other female. "Erica." He pointed behind him with a shrug. "Samara." I assumed she was Lanir's mate. After Vitri introduced us, he ushered Tori forward. She hesitated, narrowing her eyes at me before approaching when Erica moved to Ryth without hesitation.

"Let them sit," Ilk said, halting my movement as I reached out my hand to connect with Tori's head. "It's tough on them." He said something to the females in their language, and they sat on the flat rocks and beckoned Ryth and me to do the same.

I sat cross-legged and watched as Tori's gaze dropped into my lap. She made a sound with her tongue against her cheek and turned her head away as shame filled me. They were wearing clothes, and even Vitri was wearing a loincloth.

I'd get something from Ilk so the females wouldn't be bothered by my nudity.

"Sorry," I muttered and ducked my head against my chest.

Tori looked at me as she sighed and mumbled something in response. I wouldn't have been able to understand her even if I had heard her. With another sigh, she tapped her head and leaned forward. I glanced at Ryth. He already had his fingers on Erica's head, and her eyes shifted rapidly back and forth under her closed eyelids. I pressed my fingers to Tori's head and waited for her to close her eyes before reading her.

Absorbing language takes only a matter of seconds for the basics, minutes to get more in-depth, and longer if we wanted all the gestures and slang that came with it. With enough time, I could get her memories, too, but I didn't need those, only enough to communicate. I didn't think Vitri would appreciate it if I invaded his mate's mind like that. No matter how laid back he was, he was still protective over her.

Tori moaned quietly as my heart ached for a mate of my own.

After a few minutes, I withdrew my hand and held an arm out to steady Tori, where she sat as she swayed. She kept her eyes closed, and her breathing was shallow for a few moments before she took some deep, steadying breaths. Vitri came behind her at the same moment Ilk moved behind Erica, and in unison, both females leaned back against their mates and sighed contently.

My chest ached again.

Erica was the first to open her eyes. I suspected Tori was also fine as a small smile played on her lips while Vitri whispered something in her ear.

"Can you understand me?" Erica asked.

Ryth nodded, and I answered, "Yes."

She clapped her hands together. "Brilliant! Doesn't matter that I've seen it before. It's still an impressive skill."

"Is Sahcor here?" Ryth asked, and he pushed himself to his feet. His eyes were averted from where the females leaned into the touches of our brothers, and I suspected he was feeling the same waves of jealousy I was.

There was a beat of tense silence before Vitri answered, "Sahcor came to us the day before yesterday. His mate, Misha, was taken by the Ghaal. He hasn't left the cliff face since, where he can see the colony." Erica made a whimpering noise while Tori pushed herself to her feet, shoved away from Vitri, and walked away. Vitri's expression was grim. "Tori blames herself," he said simply before going after her.

Ilk helped Erica to her feet and placed an arm protectively around her shoulders. "The Ghaal put some sort of tracking device in Misha's arm. Sahcor and Misha tried to isolate themselves and set traps, but the Ghaal was waiting them out. They threatened to kill Sahcor, and Misha allowed herself to be taken to protect him." Erica shook her head sadly as Ilk spoke. "He wanted to sacrifice himself so she could get away, but she wouldn't let him."

"Why didn't they kill him anyway?" Ryth asked, and Erica gasped. I glared at him. The females were sensitive—he shouldn't be so careless with his words.

Ilk's lips twisted together in a pained expression. "From what Sahcor has told us, apparently, they implied to Misha they still have intentions to use us. To use the human females to lure us to them and then try to force us to mate with them since we wouldn't mate with each other."

"Sahcor wants to storm the colony now," Erica added and crossed her arms protectively over her chest. "We managed to convince him to wait until we were all together, including you both, so we could make a plan."

"Make a plan to rescue the females?" I couldn't help it. I was in my head again, thinking about mating. The Ghaal always worked in sixes. Six Synths, six human females—four claimed by my brothers. Two left. Between Ryth and me, we both had a chance to claim a mate of our own.

If the females would have us. We'd never force them.

"And take down the Ghaal." There was an edge to Ilk's voice as though he wasn't sure if this was the way he wanted this to end. But the Ghaal had proven over and over again they would stop at nothing to bring back their species on this planet. The Ghaal who had fled the planet a generation ago to find a new home had never returned and couldn't now even if they wanted to—no one knew where they were or if they had succeeded. Since being cut off from intergalactic trade and communication, the Ghaal had no way of knowing.

They created us—that failed—and then they turned to hiring pirates to kidnap innocent species.

They now had the humans here and were so close to their goal.

But we couldn't let them finish.

Ilk wasn't violent, but none of us were if we could avoid it. My gaze flickered to where Lanir sat in the near distance. Samara leaned back against him as she looked up at his face, laughing about something. Lanir's lip was twisted into a near-smirk. He'd been pushed into being violent when we had escaped and was tortured more than the rest of us by the Ghaal when he'd been the first to show signs of turning. I'd seen him when he was pushed to the edge. I'd felt those surges of rage myself.

We never wanted to kill or harm for the sake of it. I'd taken out my share of Ghaal while we were escaping, and it wasn't something I was proud of or particularly enjoyed.

But to save the females and end this, we may have no choice.

CHAPTER 5

ELDICH

Sahcor couldn't wait. He needed to make sure his mate was safe, and I didn't blame him.

He approached Ilk shortly after we had arrived and jabbed his finger against Ilk's chest. "Either you agree to let me go tonight, or I go anyway," Sahcor snarled out.

The females were standing back and watched the exchange with wide eyes. I agreed with Sahcor but hesitated to point out that our brother, Ilk, was practically made of stone now after living in the mountains all these years. I doubted Sahcor could move him if he didn't want to be moved.

"If the Ghaal know we're coming—"

"They'll know we're coming *anyway,*" Sahcor burst out, throwing his arms up. "Think, Ilk, *think about it.* We already know they had intentions to use *us,* and they're using Misha and the other two females to bait us all. They want *all of us* in captivity."

"What exactly do you intend to do?"

Sahcor stilled and seemed to be centering his thoughts. "I'll go into the colony. I know where the lab is. I've spent many nights exploring the colony over the years."

Ilk snarled and closed the gap between them. "We never discussed you entering the colony when we made our plans."

Sahcor didn't blink. "I didn't ask you. I did what I thought was right. One day, we'd need to know the colony's layout, and now, thanks to me, we do." He glanced at Vitri and Lanir. "None of us knew the layout before. We weren't even kept in the colony."

Ilk's jaw tensed as if he was grinding his teeth.

Erica's voice was small as she spoke up. "He's not wrong, Ilk. That information will be useful."

Ilk rounded on her but didn't growl or snarl, only stared her down as she held his gaze determinedly. She wasn't afraid of him, and she shouldn't be. Ilk could get angry, but he'd never hurt her. She was his mate. They held tense eye contact for a moment, a thousand things unsaid and perhaps previously discussed between them rushing through the silence.

"I'll go in, check Misha and the others are okay, and leave." Slowly, Ilk straightened and turned to stare at Sahcor as he spoke, as if he didn't believe a word he said. Sahcor held up his hands in defeat. "I won't try to break her out. You have my word." A low growl rumbled through his chest, and his eyes filled with pain. "It'll kill me to leave her there, but I will, for the greater good. I just need to know she's okay."

No one was asking the question *what if she's not okay?* We were all holding on to the knowledge of the Ghaal's desperation to replenish their species and that they wouldn't dare kill Misha or any of the females. *They need six.*

But the Ghaal would know we'd be coming for the females, and they were relying on it.

"I'll go with him." On an impulse, I spoke up and stepped toward Ilk. Ilk's eyes narrowed as he took me in. I mirrored Sahcor's previous gesture and held my hands up between us. "I'll make sure we're in and out, and if it's too dangerous to go in, we'll come back."

I wanted to add that I didn't know these females, and I had no stake in this. But it was an outright lie and one that Ilk would pick up on immediately. There's no way he missed the longing looks I'd given him and Erica and my other brothers when they were with their females. I wanted what they had, and my chance for it was being held in *that lab*.

The desire to see them clawed at me and I glanced at Ryth, certain he was going to volunteer too, but he remained silent.

What would my female see when she saw me? Would we have an instant connection? Would she trust me to free her from the hell she was in?

"I'm going too." Tori stepped forward, only to have Vitri step immediately behind her.

The vines that wrapped around his arms quivered as if he was resisting the urge to tie Tori up and keep her near him. "Absolutely not."

She rounded on him and shoved at his chest. "I should never have let her out of my *sight*. It's my fault she was taken. I need to make sure she's okay."

"Sahcor and Eldich will check she's okay. Then come back and report to us." Vitri grabbed her hands as she went to shove him again and held her still.

"That's not good enough." The crack in her voice had Vitri dropping her hands. He scooped her toward him, wrapped the vines that ran off his spine around her waist, and held her close.

Tori struggled for a moment, ceasing her movements only when he grabbed her chin and made her look at him. "I can't put you in danger."

Her eyes swam with emotion. "You may not have a choice. We may even need to *be* bait ourselves to get the Ghaal to let their guard down."

Vitri snarled, loud enough for Tori to recoil even as she was bound by him. "*Never.*"

"This isn't the time," Ilk roared before he turned back to Sahcor. "Fine. You go tonight, check their location and health, and leave immediately. Do you understand?"

"*Understood.*" Sahcor ground the word out between clenched teeth.

I nodded, trying to keep my expression passive.

There were two unclaimed females there, and perhaps one of them would like me.

And I was going to meet them tonight.

CHAPTER 6

AMY

The time passed slowly.

Once a day, we were taken by the Ghaal into the lab, and after the first time, I stopped struggling. There was no point anymore. All they seemed to be doing was testing our temperature at this stage, and occasionally, they'd place a strange instrument against my stomach, probably checking out my womb or something. I didn't ask.

Even if they randomly decided they would answer questions now, I wasn't sure I wanted to know.

Misha seemed certain her Synth alien boyfriend

would be coming to our rescue and that he would have gone to his brothers for help. They knew about Tegan and me because Misha had told them about us after she'd seen us in stasis before she escaped.

This was the third time she'd been in the Ghaal's captivity, and she still fought them, determined to make every move they made difficult. The Ghaal showed patience with her, being gentler than I remembered they had been with us in the beginning. Perhaps they realized how easily we could be injured and could be killed and didn't want to risk us so easily this time. The thought made my stomach churn because it made me think of Becca, but I filed the information away. Because if they didn't want to kill us, then perhaps we could use that hesitation against them.

If we were given the chance.

They took Misha more often than they took Tegan and me, and every time, she screamed at them to remove the implant they'd put in her arm. After the fourth time she came back into our cell, she was cupping her hand over her stomach, and her face was twisted into an expression I couldn't read.

"What's wrong?" I asked. I stood from where I'd been next to Tegan and crossed the cell to meet Misha halfway.

She glanced down at her stomach and then up at me. "I'm pregnant."

"*What?*" Tegan scrambled to her feet. "They did this to you? I thought you said we were safe until they had all six of us together." She ran her hands into her hair, grabbing her blonde locks and twisting as agony crossed her features. "I don't want to be impregnated with an alien baby."

"Shh," Misha shushed her, grabbed her shoulder, and placed her other hand gently over Tegan's mouth. "Stay calm, *please.* It's not a Ghaal baby."

"You mean…" I stepped up next to her as she released Tegan, who continued to watch Misha with wide eyes. "You and your alien boyfriend…"

"Sahcor." Misha almost smiled, then her gaze moved around the cell, and her smile fell. "Sahcor is the father."

"Won't the Ghaal try to…" I gestured to her stomach, unwilling to utter the words lest I put a jinx or something on her. Misha cupped her hands protectively over her stomach, catching my drift without me needing to say it as I continued, "Because it's not a Ghaal?"

Misha shook her head. "The Synths are a combination of Ghaal and lab-created DNA. The Ghaal *wanted* the Synths to breed. I guess breeding with us is the next best thing." She looked down sadly. "My baby has Ghaal DNA in it. If it grows up and breeds with a full-blooded Ghaal… you see how they think. They won't risk the baby's life. It's too precious to them."

"And to you?" I offered gently.

Her smile was weak. "This baby is mine and Sahcor's. Whatever the Ghaal think, they're wrong. They can't have it. Sahcor will come for us." She moved to the cell's back wall and eased herself onto the floor, picking up a piece of the food we left for her. "I know he will."

Sleep didn't come easy at the best of times in this cell, so when a hissing sound could be heard over the howling of the usual winds at night, I was jolted from my uneasy slumber.

"*Misha.*"

This time, the hiss was a voice, and it was filled with urgency. My hand flung out to wake Misha, but instead, I slapped the cold wall behind me. Misha was already standing, her shadow stretched out behind her in the light cast across the cell from the moon outside. I stood and stepped forward just as Misha bolted across the floor. She flung herself up against the wall and reached for the window. Large hands came between the bars and grabbed her face.

"Sahcor!"

I shook Tegan to wake her and pressed a finger to her lips to crush any questions she may have.

Cautiously, we moved toward the window but stood back from where Misha's sobs were audible over the quiet, reassuring whispers of Sahcor. Apparently, her alien boyfriend *had* come for her.

For *us.*

"I knew you'd come for me. I knew it. *I knew it.*"

"Of course, I came, Misha, but please listen. I can't stay long."

"The others, are they safe?"

Sahcor pressed a kiss to her lips. "My mate, always worrying about others. The females… Samara, Tori, and Erica are safe with us." Misha let out a sob at this and nodded before she kissed him again.

Sahcor—his skin a deep gray with a bright purple pattern dappled across it—looked behind Misha at Tegan and me. He was lying on his stomach next to the small window and had reached through the bars to touch Misha's face. Next to him, on his hands and knees, was another alien, and I could only assume he was another one of the Synths Misha told us about. He looked different from Sahcor, and while it was difficult to tell the exact color of his skin in the dull light, it was a lighter and warmer shade than Sahcor's, of that I was sure. His hair was pulled back into a ponytail, and his bright eyes shone in the light.

And he stared directly at me.

He didn't blink and barely moved as Sahcor

whispered to Misha. I struggled to concentrate on listening to Sahcor talk as I held the other alien's eye contact. "I had to come just to make sure you were okay. We can't take you, not tonight, but we're making a plan."

"Sahcor, please, I have to tell you somethi—"

"Stay strong, my mate. We will be coming for you."

"Sahcor," the alien next to him spoke, and my lip twitched with the urge to smile at his voice's deep, soothing rumble. He pressed a hand on Sahcor's shoulder. "We need to make sure the other females are okay too."

Sahcor growled at him but lowered Misha to the cell floor. As he shuffled to the side, he allowed the other alien to lie down next to him. Misha kept her hands gripped in Sahcor's and tilted her head toward the alien as she held my eye contact, encouraging me to approach him.

He never once took his gaze from mine, and I couldn't tear my eyes away from the intensity of his stare. It was like he was hypnotizing me or being hypnotized *by* me. He reached through the bars, I stepped toward the window, and ignored Tegan as she hissed, "*Don't.*"

I took his hand and simply held it as his long fingers curled around mine. My hand fit snugly into his palm, and still, his eyes never left my face. "Eldich."

It took me a moment to realize this must be his name. "I'm Amy, and this is Tegan."

"Amy…" he whispered my name as if it were poetry, and I released an unsteady breath.

Holy crap, this was neither the time nor the place to be seduced, but damn, the way he was *looking* at me was something else. I don't think I've ever been looked at like that. I studied his face as he watched me. He didn't look *unlike* a human, at least in his facial features. But the color of his skin and hair and the way his long fingers wrapped around my hand were only a hint of his size and enough to remind me he was an *alien.* He wasn't checking me out in a lurid way but staring into my eyes as if trying to convey some message without words.

Whatever it was, I'd be happy to stare into those eyes until I figured it out. *Damn.*

"Sahcor," Misha whispered urgently as she reached up to Sahcor's face again and stood on her toes. "I'm—"

There was a sudden burst of angry shouts, and Eldich withdrew his arms from the cell. The brush of his fingers from my hand felt like a loss before throwing me one last longing look before he went to stand. When Sahcor didn't move, Eldich gripped his shoulder and shook him. "We must go."

"Misha…"

"Sahcor, we must go *now.*"

Misha sobbed as Sahcor pulled away. "I will

come back for you, my mate."

Their footsteps thudded as they disappeared into the night, followed by more steps I could only assume was the Ghaal. There was an exchange of annoyed shouting in their strange, clicky language as we sunk back against the wall. Misha had her arms wrapped around her stomach. I draped an arm over her shoulder and pulled her against me as she cried quietly. It was one thing to be kept captive, but it was another to have a loved one *so close* and not be able to go with them. It seemed Sahcor and Eldich had simply come to make sure we were okay—at least as okay as we could be—and while it seemed a lot of danger to face for simply that, I was grateful for it.

As Misha snuggled against me, she sighed and wiped away her tears.

Tegan nudged my elbow. I faced her as she asked, "What was that all about?"

I hoped the dim lighting was enough to cover the flush in my cheeks. "What?"

She rolled her eyes. "You and that weird alien making goo-goo eyes at each other." Her face twisted as if disgusted, and I pressed my lips together.

"Don't be so quick to judge. Those aliens will be the ones to save us."

She made a little *harrumph* sound before she sunk against the cell's corner. I noticed she was leaning slightly away from me, and I frowned. Usually, we stay close to keep warm. "Save *you* maybe… he barely even looked at me."

My brows drew together as she turned away to go back to sleep, and I glanced back at Misha and watched her for a moment as her breathing evened out as she, too, drifted off, still tucked under my arm.

Why would Tegan be upset Eldich was looking at me? They would come to save us all, not just Misha and me.

Glancing at Tegan again, I thought about how different our lives must have been on Earth. She was beautiful, popular, the envy of all the girls, and desired by all the boys. An absolute cliché. Before we'd been frozen, I'd gotten to know her as well as I could, but beyond our shared circumstances, she barely opened up to me. It was over a week after we were first put in the cell together before she'd look at me, preferring to speak to Monica and Luna, women equally as beautiful as Tegan. I remember being frustrated more than jealous, as it was hardly the situation to be keeping to cliques. But old habits die hard, I guessed, and Tegan simply fell into patterns that made her comfortable. I couldn't blame her for trying to find comfort in our situation.

But here, like all of us, all that Tegan had on Earth was gone. Everything she considered her identity was wiped away in a single moment. But there was more to her. I was sure of it. She'd become so wrapped up in the things she *did* that she was lost without them. Of course, I sympathized with her, but all of us were in the same situation. We'd all been taken from our homes and everything we knew. We all had lives before this place—lives we would *never* get back.

Twelve cycles of the sun.

It seemed impossible, and I leaned my head against the cool wall behind me, wondering what my niece looked like now and if she was enjoying high school.

Despite all these thoughts that should have me drowning in melancholy, I couldn't help but smile as I ducked my head against my chest at the thought of Eldich. I'd never been looked at like that before, and I wanted him to come back. I wanted to learn about who he was beyond someone who was apparently *struck* by me.

Managing to stifle a giggle—which seemed absurd given our predicament—I sighed.

If Tegan wanted to be jealous of an alien giving me attention, there wasn't much I could do about that. Maybe it would give her something to focus on other than where we were.

Images of Eldich's hand encompassing mine snuck into my thoughts and stayed there as I drifted back to sleep.

CHAPTER 7

ELDICH

We couldn't return to Ilk's until after first light, not until we were certain we weren't being followed. It was a close call visiting the females, and the Ghaal had come out of nowhere and surrounded us. We noticed them only seconds before it was too late.

We crouched in the bushes on the sandy soil near the cliff's edge overlooking the beach and the colony, and I whispered to Sahcor, "They weren't trying to kill us."

"No…" Sahcor muttered back as his gaze scanned the area surrounding us through the darkness. "They meant to capture us."

"How do you know for sure?"

"Misha told me." Before I could ask how Misha knew, he added, "The Ghaal told Misha."

So that's why we were still alive and why the Ghaal had left us alone all these years. They had intentions of using us again for breeding. However, not with each other this time but with the human females. Our offspring would contain the stronger Synth DNA, and enough Ghaal if they interbred the following generation, the offspring from there would be almost completely Ghaal. They would plan to raise them without our or the females' input. I'm sure of it.

Six female humans, six males Synths.

They'd have an excellent start at rebuilding their numbers.

"They can't possibly believe they can capture us all? We're stronger than them."

Sahcor's eyes darkened. I didn't like this side of him as it was unfamiliar to me. But Misha was his mate, and she was being held captive, which forced his protective instincts to take over. "They know our weakness."

I didn't need to ask what because I knew too.

The females.

Amy.

She was beautiful, and from one touch of her smooth skin, I knew she would be my mate. There was no fear in her eyes when she looked at me as there was with Tegan. Tegan was slender and frail, but Amy was voluptuous. She would birth strong offspring, and my cock ached at the thought of how she would feel under my hands.

I can imagine how her thighs will feel when she parts them for me.

With a grunt, I cut off the string of distracting thoughts. They weren't helping right now.

We were to return to Ilk's and create a plan to not only rescue the captured females but take down the Ghaal once and for all. The thought settled a heavy weight in my stomach. While I knew they had proven themselves unworthy of life, it still felt wrong to be deciding on what would ultimately be a violent action and wipe a species from the face of the planet.

"Do you have any ideas about the plan?" I whispered to Sahcor, and he nodded.

"Some."

The weight in my stomach eased. I shouldn't be relying on him so much to do this planning, but he had always been better at thinking rationally and logically than me, and perhaps I was looking for an excuse to mentally check out.

Because instead of thinking about the plan, I was thinking about Amy.

And how I planned to sneak back and see her again.

In the evening, I planned to leave Ilk's cave under the guise of going out to hunt gorae for us.

The day had been spent gathering supplies and exchanging ideas on how to take down the Ghaal. We had no weapons apart from spears and knives, having refused to take any of their technology with us when we left. And while their technology was unreliable, from Sahcor's telling us about when they took Misha, it seemed they still possessed the weapons designed to take us down. Small enough to fit in the palm of their hands, a stab would inject a serum into our bodies and begin shutting down our created Synth DNA and ultimately kill us.

These weapons didn't work against the Ghaal, but for us, it was a death sentence. Of course, they didn't create us without a failsafe to get rid of us if needed. It was only by surprise and sheer force—and Lanir's absolute rage—that we managed to escape at all.

I didn't want to admit to my brothers how the prospect of this attack made me nervous and churned sickness in my stomach. We weren't designed for war, not really. Our strength and speed were purely to produce advantageous offspring, and these days, we used these gifts for survival, not to fight.

We were untrained, outnumbered, and outgunned.

But there was determination, and it was enough to spur us on to keep trying. If we could reduce the Ghaal numbers enough to make it an even fight, we would have more than a chance.

Then we'd have the upper hand.

"What about the eye-lakes?" Samara spoke up, and her small voice carried across the group as we sat in a circle around a fire.

"Eylaks," Lanir grunted out. Samara nodded and patted his arm as she grinned at him.

"What the fuck are eylaks?" Tori looked between them, then at Vitri, urging someone to explain. I noticed immediately she didn't like being out of the loop and needed to know what was happening at all times. Yet, if *Vitri* asked something of her while we were working to gather supplies, she would glare at him, yet do what he needed without questioning him.

Not as much as she questioned everyone else anyway.

Samara's nose scrunched as she pulled a face, and her fingers tightened where she still held onto Lanir's arm. "They're these horrible giant roach things that live in the sand. They have barbs that contain poison of some sort. Apparently, it would be enough to kill us. It was certainly enough to knock Lanir out for a day and a night."

Lanir's lip lifted into a snarl. I doubt he liked being reminded of his weakness, but he said nothing.

"Would this venom kill the Ghaal?" Erica asked.

Ilk nodded. "Almost definitely."

"Brilliant," Tori said, smiling at Samara. "Look at you, plotting deaths like an evil queen."

Samara threw an empty water bag at Tori as she smirked.

"They want us all alive, so I think we're going to need to use that," Ilk said.

"You might need to use us as a distraction," Erica added.

This was met with a growl from Ilk, and the sound dominated any chatter that remained after Erica's comment. "Not going to happen."

Her brows pulled together as she poked at his thigh. "We've been over this. You may not have a choice. They're hardly going to buy it if you lot just wander into the colony like, *oh, we've decided to surrender.* Physically, you're a threat, and they might take you down if they're jumpy. But us..." she indicated herself, Tori, and Samara, "... we're more precious to them and weaker than they are."

"And therefore vulnerable," Vitri growled out.

"I think that's the point," Tori added.

"Do you have a better idea about how we can get into where Misha and the others are being held?"

Erica challenged Vitri, and Tori raised her eyebrows at him as if willing him to answer with something better.

Through gritted teeth, he replied, "Not yet."

Shortly after, I declared I would go hunting. Ilk nodded and stood to hunt himself, and we headed in different directions.

But I needed to check on Amy.

I wouldn't try to rescue her. I owed Ilk that much, and we had an agreement. Although, it wouldn't be easy to leave her there again. Last night, I'd had to physically drag Sahcor away from Misha, and although he *knew* we needed to go, you simply can't battle love and instinct with logic. His instincts were taking over, and his every nerve screamed at him not to leave his mate there for another minute.

It would be easier for me to sneak into the colony undetected than it was for Sahcor and me together, and I needed to talk to Amy. I needed to hear her voice say my name, make her smile, cup her cheek in my palm, tell her she'd be safe soon, and I would look after her.

It was pitch black by the time I reached the colony's edge, and I kept low, ducking between the sparse tree trunks and harsh undergrowth. These were not the same trees as in the woodlands where I'd resided these past years, and I didn't blend in but instead relied on the darkness to cover me. Our adaption to our environments wasn't instant, and I couldn't simply change my color on the spot to suit my location. The physical changes for survival happened over time, and the only change that was quicker was our body's desire to change into female in order to mate.

With the human females, I hoped that wouldn't be an issue. It was only when my brothers and I were sectioned in close quarters alone together that it became a challenge—before it became impossible—to resist the change.

As expected, Ghaal sentries were spotted around the lab building, but once again, the rear window that backed against the woodlands was mostly clear. I remembered my conversation with Sahcor about how they were planning on taking us alive and thought perhaps the lack of guards was a trap.

I wasn't stupid, but I was stubborn, and I wanted to see Amy.

I *needed* to see her.

I'd noticed them approaching last night and heard the telltale cracking of small branches and twigs even over the winds. The winds hadn't picked up yet and, therefore, couldn't be used to cover the sounds of approach. I could do it again, and I'd hear the Ghaal before they got too close.

I only needed a few minutes, seconds even, if that's all I could get.

Crouching low, I moved forward on my stomach and shuffled the remainder of the way before I gripped the cool bars of the cell window and peeked in. Amy was in the corner, squashed between Misha and Tegan. Misha's arm was thrown around Amy's midriff while Amy rested her cheek on Misha's head. A sting hit my heart at the sight of them comforting each other, even in sleep, and I didn't want to disturb them.

This was selfish of me.

My palms were on the ground, ready to push myself away, when Amy's eyes opened, and she gasped quietly. After a glance at Misha, I shook my head—*don't wake her.* Amy nodded and held my eye contact for a moment longer before she gently shuffled from between the two girls. Misha grumbled in her sleep and slid downward, her head landing in Tegan's lap. Amy watched them for a moment before she crept the length of the cell toward me.

Standing out of my reach, Amy crossed her arms over her chest, her gaze unable to settle on my face for longer than a few seconds.

"Are you here to rescue us?" she whispered as she took another tentative step forward.

"Not yet."

But I want to, Amy. You have no idea how desperately I want you out of this place.

Her brows pulled together. "Then why are you here?" Her eyes widened. "Did something happen to one of Misha's friends?"

"Everyone is okay, but I had to see you."

She took another step closer, and every inch of space that was closed between us made my heart beat harder. One more step and I'd be able to brush my hand across her cheek, her lips…

"Why?" she asked again, and while the question was in her eyes, there was a shadow of a smile playing on her lips. "You don't know me."

"Not yet," I purred the words out, and she smiled wide then.

"Eldich…" she whispered, and I reached through the bars as she took that final step toward me. "This is all very strange."

When I reached forward and brushed my fingers across her cheek, she didn't pull away, only stared at me with questioning eyes. But there was a softness to her expression, and her eyes fluttered closed as she tilted her head into my palm. I couldn't help it. My pheromones released and increased in strength. Amy leaned into my touch, and it stirred something in me. If she wanted me as much as I wanted her, there'd be no stopping me from sinking my cock into her pretty cunt when she was free, and we were together.

"You smell good," she muttered and lifted her hand to cup it over mine. When she opened her eyes, she met my gaze. "You should leave before they come."

"I don't want to leave you here."

Amy was on her toes now with her body pressed against the cell's wall. She was barely able to see up to the bottom of the window. "Misha said Sahcor bent these bars last time to get her out."

I scowled. "I could bend the bars." I was as strong as Sahcor. I could protect Amy. Her silence asked all the questions she didn't need to voice. "Your being here is a lure. The Ghaal are setting traps."

"Can't we all just leave, run away, and never be found?"

"Misha is being tracked. Perhaps you are too…"

The thought hadn't occurred to her. It was obvious in the way her eyes widened. She dropped her hand from mine and started scouring her arms for signs of an implant.

"Amy…" When she didn't stop, I grabbed her face, gently holding her cheeks between my fingers. Her brows pulled together again, and she pouted. When I smiled, she smiled in return, although it was a sad one. "We will get you out soon, and we'll make it so the Ghaal no longer come after us."

"Are you going to kill them?"

I hesitated. What was the right answer here? Would the idea that I had thought of shedding blood make Amy fear me? Were humans a peaceful species? After a pause, I answered, "If we need to."

There was no tang to her scent after that, no additional fear beyond the fear she already felt simply by being here.

"You should leave," she said again.

"Amy—"

"*Amy.*" Amy spun around at the sound of Tegan's voice, and Misha jolted awake a second later. "What are you doing?"

"Eldich?" Misha pushed herself to her feet. "Where's Sahcor?"

"Go," Amy hissed out as she turned back to me.

"I'll come back for you." I pulled my arms from the bars and shuffled away.

Only to feel the pressure of a Ghaal's weapon at the back of my neck.

CHAPTER 8

AMY

As I stepped back from the window, there was an angry scuffling, followed by Eldich's growls and a hasty exchange in a language I didn't understand. My fingers ran through my hair, and I gripped handfuls as Misha came up behind me. "They've got him," I choked out.

Tegan screamed as a Ghaal looked through the window and offered us a horrible toothy grin before it moved away to join the group, no doubt with Eldich in tow.

"Why did he have to come back? He knew it was dangerous." I faced Misha as panic gripped my heart. The feeling spread and sent waves of sickness to my stomach and tears to my eyes. "Why did he do it?"

"Did he tell you the plan?"

"No." I shook my head and squeezed my eyes shut for a moment. "He just said he needed to see me, but he couldn't break us out yet, not until they'd taken care of the Ghaal. He said they knew us being here was intended as a trap."

"Then why did he come?" Tegan snapped.

"He came for you," Misha said as her gaze fell on the now-empty window, and the winds started to pick up.

"Why? I asked him why, and he couldn't tell me."

Misha sighed, grabbed my hand, and led me back to the corner where we slept. Tegan followed, and we were silent for a few moments as we arranged ourselves until we were as comfortable as we could get. But I couldn't get comfortable. My skin tingled where Eldich had touched me, and I wanted to rush to the window and scream his name as if that would bring him back.

"Synths were designed for breeding," Misha started, looking between us. "For mating. Their instinct to find a partner is strong, so strong, in fact, it overrides almost everything else when it's in full swing." A smile quirked the corner of her lips. "Sahcor made his share of stupid decisions while we were together, especially when we first spent time with each other, before we… you know."

"Did the *wild thang?*" I offered with a watery chuckle.

Misha smirked. "Right." Then she sighed again. "They're adaptive, you know. Not just to their environments, but they can change gender. That's what they were designed to do. Alone together long enough, one or more of them would change. So, because we're compatible with the Ghaal, we're compatible with the Synths too. They're just responding to instinct. An instinct that's been more than bred into them. It's been *designed* into their DNA." She looked at me as if she were willing me to understand. "Eldich obviously feels some connection to you, and because of that, he'd struggle to resist his instinct to mate. But that doesn't make him dangerous. He'd never hurt you. He just… likes you."

"Great." Tegan let out a huff. "So, if we're rescued from these aliens who want to breed us, we're falling right into the arms of *different* aliens who want to breed us."

Misha's spine stiffened where she sat next to me. "The Synths would never force you."

"How strong are these instincts exactly?" Tegan countered, and Misha's stare was cold.

"What are you implying?"

Tegan shook her head and looked at her hands on her lap. "If the Ghaal created them for breeding…

all I'm saying is maybe they can be programmed to fuck or something. Eldich may be trapped here as a victim like us, but for all we know, he could be *used*." There was something in her face when Tegan met my eyes that sent a shiver down my spine. "The Ghaal want stronger babies, and they might force Eldich to force us."

"That won't happen," Misha said, but her voice wavered, and Tegan nodded stiffly as if her concerns had been validated.

"Sure," she scoffed before she turned her back to us. "You sound really certain of that."

Sleep was almost impossible, and the heavy weight of worry in my chest had solidified into something that physically dragged me down. I was tired, and my face felt puffy when I rubbed my eyes in the morning, awoken from whatever semblance of sleep I'd managed by sunlight streaming through the window.

Scowling, I silently cursed the window. This entire place was set up as a trap, and we were the bait.

The door at the end of the hall slid open, and three Ghaal entered, chatting excitedly amongst themselves. When they reached the cell, they turned to us, each sporting equally unsettling grins.

"This couldn't have turned out any better," one said, hovering his hand over the silver ball that unlocked the cell. "We thought the Synth who impregnated you would be the first one to come back. But you're already pregnant, and his mating instincts won't switch to another so easily." He waved a hand at Misha before turning his cold gaze to me. "But the other Synth, he must be keen on one of you two."

A shudder ran down my spine, and I stiffened as I was shoved to the side.

"It was me," Tegan announced as she stood in front of me. "He came back to see me."

My jaw dropped. I knew Tegan about as well as could be expected given our circumstances, but I *never* would have thought of her as the self-sacrificing type.

I couldn't let her do it.

"No." I grabbed Tegan's arm, and she immediately tried to yank it from my grip. "It was me. The Synth wants me."

The Ghaal glanced at each other, smirking as Tegan hissed out at me, "What are you doing?"

"You can't do this. It's okay. He won't hurt me."

Tegan shook her head rapidly, keeping her tone hushed. "You don't *know* that. Maybe I won't engage his instincts or whatever."

The cell door slid open, and Misha grabbed us both and tugged us backward away from the Ghaal as they entered. "It doesn't matter. We'll take you both. He'll choose."

"He won't hurt them," Misha said, snarling as she was forced away from us with her arm twisted painfully behind her back when she fought.

"You carry a Ghaal child. Don't make me hurt you."

"It's not a Ghaal, it's a *Synth!*" she cried and kicked out, effectively lifting herself from the floor as the Ghaal shifted his weight to hold her back.

A scuffle broke out as both Tegan and I tried to get to Misha, and Misha fought equally hard to get to us. I had barely a moment to consider the bond we'd formed—one born from circumstances and desperation. It was how I'd been with Becca, and my heart simply couldn't take watching history repeating itself. With every fiber of my being, I wished for these women to be safe, and I'd fight for them as viciously as I would my own flesh and blood.

The Ghaal outnumbered us as more flooded into the cell, and in less than a minute, they had Tegan and I held in similar grips to Misha, with our arms tucked behind our backs, and we were forced to walk toward the cell door. Misha was shoved back against the wall, and the door slammed in her face and locked before she could get out. Her fingers wrapped around the cool bars, and she shook them, yelling at the Ghaal. "Bring them back! You don't have six. *You don't have six.*"

The Ghaal paused in their step, and I drew in a shuddering breath. Misha had reminded them of their superstition, one they apparently held above almost everything else. One of them turned to her and bared his teeth in a sneer. "Torturing the Synth will take time. By the time he's ready, we'll have you all."

Misha's shouts were cut out as the door closed behind us, and once again, Tegan and I were led into the lab.

CHAPTER 9

ELDICH

Her scent reached me before I saw her, and I tugged against the restraints the Ghaal had placed me in. Amy was brought into the lab with the other female—Tegan—and I couldn't drag my eyes from Amy and followed her path as she was walked between and around the equipment. She glanced at me quickly and shook her head ever so slightly before she looked back at the floor. My brows drew together, and I didn't understand. But I said nothing. Instead, I followed her lead, stared at the lab's floor, and tried not to imagine what was the cause of the dark stains that dotted it.

I knew they'd held species here, anything they could get their hands on. I knew there'd been experiments, and I squeezed my eyes shut, willing away the images of what they wanted to do to Amy.

I wouldn't let them.

I hadn't fought them when they led me here, knowing that Amy would be safer if I didn't fight too hard. The weapon they had held to my neck could kill me in a matter of minutes if it broke the skin, but for the first time in a long time, I had something to fight for.

The chance of a mate.

Her.

When they'd first captured me, I'd managed to knock the weapon from a Ghaal's hand when he thought I had become compliant, and spun on my heel, grabbed his head between my hands, and twisted until his neck snapped. When his body hit the ground with an empty thunk, I'd stood frozen for a moment too long. The move had been so foreign to me, but I thought of Amy in trouble, and instantly, I'd done what needed to be done to protect her.

The severity with which these instincts took over and my responding violence concerned me.

A group of Ghaal had surrounded me, and half of them bared the weapons that would take me down.

"This is ridiculous," one of them hissed out of the corner of his mouth. "Why can't we just kill him?

Look what he just did to Henk."

"Rah wants him alive. A lot was put into creating them, so we may as well use them."

When I growled and changed my stance, ready to attack, the first Ghaal to speak threw a worried glance at me. "He'll kill us if given the chance."

"So, don't give him the chance."

They closed in, and I couldn't have avoided the weapons any longer. Taking one out would leave me exposed to another, and it would only take a single stab to take me down. I'd lowered my hands, dropped to my knees, and allowed them to restrain me.

Now, I was in the lab with Amy and Tegan.

I dared another glance at Amy and snarled when I saw she was being tied. All three of us were bound on chairs big enough to hold me, so the females looked small and vulnerable in them. The chairs faced each other, and my gaze shifted to Tegan. She was visibly trembling, but when her eyes met mine, there was a flicker of determination there.

They were expecting the worst.

But they did not know what the worst could be.

"How will we know which one it is?" a Ghaal muttered.

Fear made me jolt in the chair, realizing their intentions, and I snarled, "Leave them alone."

There was a chuckle. "Maybe he'll go for either. He seems pretty agitated already."

"It's possible, but there'll be one he'll respond to stronger. Easy enough to figure out."

Tegan and Amy glanced at each other with identical expressions of concern and fear. They couldn't understand what the Ghaal were saying, but I doubted they needed to. They'd seen and experienced enough to know any time they were in this lab was dangerous. Amy tried to stretch her fingers toward Tegan to take her hand or offer a comforting touch but couldn't move enough with the restraints. Pain tugged at my heart again. My future mate was so thoughtful, and here she was in danger because of me.

A voice in my head told me the Ghaal would have tried something regardless of my presence, but my brothers and I were relying on their need to make sure they had all six females before they started attempting to impregnate them. I squeezed my eyes shut, hoping Ilk and the others didn't wait too long to attempt rescue. I shouldn't have come here. But the pull to Amy was something I hadn't experienced since my brothers and I were locked up together, and my body had called me to mate.

My presence here meant they were going to try something else, something new, and I had an idea where this was going.

They wished to engage my instinct and force a mating.

I had failed to fight my instincts to go see Amy.

What if I failed to fight them and hurt her in the process?

An agonized groan was torn from my throat, and Amy looked at me in alarm before she returned her gaze to the floor.

The Ghaal laughed. "I think he's just figured out what's going on, Rah."

"Took him long enough. Give me that."

One held his hand out while another slapped a simple blade into his palm.

"Touch them and die," I snarled out the words, and the smallest hesitation from the Ghaal made my lips curl into a sneer.

They still feared us.

But his hesitation was short-lived, and he swiped the blade down Tegan's arm. She cried out and tried to jerk away from them, and I growled, tugging at my restraints. There was no winning in this. If I managed to control my reaction, they would only continue torturing them. If I hid my desire for Amy, they would take it out on Tegan. If my want slipped through, Amy would be their victim.

I met Amy's eyes, pleading with her without words.

What do I do?

And almost as if we had a link, an understanding that didn't need words, Amy sighed quietly with her eyes still on mine and inclined her head. It was the smallest motion, but I understood.

It's okay.

She wouldn't want Tegan to take any punishment intended for her.

My future mate is so noble. Do I even deserve her?

My thoughts were interrupted when the Ghaal approached Amy. He paused as he was interrupted by a Ghaal standing behind me. "You are a hypocrite, Rah."

Rah stilled and slowly turned his head to face the one who had spoken. "Something to say, El?"

"You refuse to impregnate the females until we have six, but you'll gladly stimulate the Synth to do it for us. Where do your loyalties to our beliefs begin and end exactly?"

Rah stared at him, and I watched his face until my skin prickled with discomfort, even though his focus was over my shoulder. "We are bound by our beliefs, and we know what happens if we break them. The Synths..." he jabbed at me with his foot, "... while tools, are living beings with free will, but will, we can crack. They are not bound like us."

"We're wasting time!" El snapped, and I heard a shuffle as others moved away from him, no doubt desperate not to be near him as he spoke up to Rah. "There are so few of us left. Be damned with the outdated superstitions... let's impregnate the females we have *now.*"

"Do you not recall what happened last time we abandoned our beliefs?"

"Of course, I do—"

"Then be quiet, or your only purpose will be fertilizer for our crops."

Amy was watching the exchange and glanced at me as she sought clarity to words she couldn't understand. There was nothing I could tell her, not here and now. Amy held my eye contact right up until the moment another Ghaal stepped forward and swiped the blade so it sliced into her skin. Her eyes squeezed shut, and she clamped her mouth closed, but her pain escaped on a whimper she couldn't control. A roar left me, and with a surge of strength, I pulled at the binds as I tried to stand. The chair creaked, one of the binds loosened slightly, and immediately, three Ghaal surrounded me and doubled down on the restraints.

"I think we found the one."

I held the gaze of the one with the knife as he smiled triumphantly. I would remember his eyes, the one the other Ghaal had called Rah.

He will *die first.*

CHAPTER
10

AMY

Eldich fought like an animal. The smallest hint of weakness showed itself in the binds that held him, and the Ghaal struggled to control him as they resecured the binds. They were apparently not prepared for the display of strength, even though it was exactly what they were trying to coax from him. I couldn't help but smirk, even as the sting in my arm throbbed where the Ghaal had cut me, and I ducked my head against my chest to hide my reaction.

This was only stage one, and it was the very *first* thing they'd done to entice an instinctual reaction from Eldich. Almost immediately, they'd lost control of him. My smirk faltered as I considered Tegan's concerns from earlier. If they managed to rile Eldich up enough, could they force him to impregnate me? How much control could they have over him then when a simple cut to my arm drove him crazy?

What would be stopping him from rampaging around and taking out every Ghaal he encountered?

Or me.

The thought stung, and I kept my head down as shame swirled within me. I didn't want to think Eldich was capable of hurting me. I didn't *believe* it. Almost as if I could feel something from him—a gentle giant. Gritting my teeth, I forced those thoughts to back off. Not only would Eldich not hurt me, but he and his brothers would ultimately *save* us.

Misha had said there were *six* Synths. Six almost unstoppable forces, all protecting the females they'd come to claim as their partners. Their *mates.* Misha was already pregnant—were the other girls pregnant too? Out there in the wilderness with their cavemen aliens? Were they happy and safe?

I risked a peek up at Eldich, and his stare burned into me as he was bound tighter against the chair Again, a tickle of heat teased my cheeks. I shouldn't care so much that Eldich had shown such interest in me, but it was difficult to stop my reaction. Back at home, if I'd stood next to Tegan in a bar or club, I'd practically be invisible to men.

But Eldich had immediately chosen *me*.

Given our predicament, these were ridiculous feelings to have, but I couldn't help them.

And it was these feelings that had me struggling against my binds as I screamed, "Stop!" as the Ghaal used the cattle prod-like weapon to shock Eldich into submission when he wouldn't stop fighting. At first, when the shock jerked his body, he only fought harder, and his eyes blazed with rage. But the Ghaal didn't remove the weapon from his skin and instead kept it there until Eldich's body was convulsing in his chair, and a slight sear formed on his skin where the weapon touched him.

"Stop it! *Stop it, you're killing him,*" I cried out and pulled harder against the restraints, ignoring how they dug into my arms.

Finally, they removed the weapon, and when Eldich slumped in his chair, they finished with the extra restraints. Eldich's eyes followed their movements, and his head lolled slightly as he tried to lift it. A dark expression crossed his face, but it changed when he looked at me, and for the first time, I knew what it felt like to have a male look at me *that way*.

Protective.

Possessive.

Before I could speak to him and ask if he was

okay, Tegan was untied and removed from her chair.

"Leave her *alone,*" I shouted and tried to kick out at the Ghaal as they walked past. But I was unable to do much, and Tegan looked back at me as she was led away, her eyes full of sympathy and concern. She and I were bound, and despite the circumstances of our connection—through trauma—we *had* connected. I could see the guilt in her eyes and hoped—that in the brief moment we looked at each other—she knew I didn't blame her for not being able to save me.

"Relax." I flinched as a Ghaal spoke to me so I could understand. "She's going back to the cell. You should be more concerned about yourself."

Tegan fought, but as usual, it was useless, and she disappeared through the door that would take her back to the cell with Misha.

The same Ghaal grabbed my chin firmly when I continued to stare where Tegan had disappeared and tilted my head so I was forced to face him. I stared determinedly into his eyes, displaying courage I wasn't feeling. "I saw you smile when the Synth fought us, female." Any façade I had dropped in that instant at the coolness of his tone, and I started to tremble under his gaze. "Don't get cocky. We're only just getting started."

He moved away from me, and I gulped in air when he was clear from my space. Looking up, I found Eldich staring at me.

"I'm sorry," I whispered. There wasn't much point in whispering. We were in such close quarters with the Ghaal in this lab they would hear everything I said anyway. But I wanted to whisper so I could at least pretend I had some semblance of control over this situation.

This was between Eldich and me and no one else.

Eldich shook his head. "Don't apologize. I should be sorry."

I wanted to ask him if the others would be coming for us, but while I'm sure the Ghaal already knew there would be something planned, I didn't want to confirm anything for them. It's best they should be left guessing. Eldich's lip twisted into a sad smile as if he could tell what I'd been thinking, and he nodded in a slight, stiff movement.

Stay strong. They'll come for us.

The connection I had to this alien man had formed faster and stronger than I would have thought possible, and while I hated everything about our situation, something about being near Eldich made it that tiny bit bearable.

But still... "You should've stayed away," I said.

There was a lopsided smile this time, and he tilted his head at me as if his answer was so obvious. "I couldn't."

There was nothing left to say. Although I had thousands of questions for him, we simply stared at each other as I tried to ignore the sound of the Ghaal gathering whatever tools they planned to use to try and get the reaction from Eldich they desired. Eldich's hair was still pulled back into a ponytail, but it was no longer neat, and strands of hair were plastered to his sweat-covered forehead. My fingers twitched as I found myself wanting to touch his skin again. The feel of the brush of his hands over mine seemed so far away. His skin was a sandy tone with long streaks of dappled white that started from his feet and followed up his strong legs and over his body. It was as though someone had spray-painted lengths of bamboo with a stencil onto his skin.

"The woodlands," he said quietly. I hastily moved my gaze from his legs back to his eyes, and my cheeks heated at having been caught letting my stare linger too long. "I look like the woodlands where I live."

"You can camouflage," I said simply, and he nodded.

I had a feeling he was talking to keep me distracted, but we both knew this conversation was going to come to an abrupt and unpleasant end very soon.

"Amy." His voice dragged me from my dark thoughts, and I focused on meeting his eyes again— bright green and full of life, concern, and a sparkle of rage. "Whatever they do, I'll make them pay."

I nodded, unable to stop my trembling lip, when

a Ghaal turned around to face me. "Adjust her chair and spread her legs."

As he gave the instruction, I was unable to control the sob that escaped, and once there was one, there were others, and soon I was a crying mess. I cried until I could barely breathe as my chair was shifted so my thighs were spread, and I was exposed to Eldich and, even worse—to the Ghaal.

Eldich didn't take his eyes from mine, although I could see the muscles in his arms as they tensed. "Amy, look at me. It's going to be okay. Just don't stop looking at me."

I nodded, even as tears streamed down my cheeks as I held his gaze, and blinked them away whenever they blurred my vision. I focused on Eldich's face and tried to remember how his hand had felt when he caressed my cheek.

And how he promised we would be rescued.

"Do you smell her, Synth? The scent from her cunt?" A Ghaal hissed in Eldich's ear.

I whimpered as Eldich tensed further, the corded muscles of his arms straining as he gripped the chair. "Don't listen to them, Amy." His eyes were still on mine, and I nodded, even as I sniffled again, the tears streaming down my cheeks.

He kept saying my name, and I knew it was to ground me. But no matter how much I tried to keep my gaze on his face, I couldn't help but flicker a glance at a Ghaal who stood over his shoulder and whispered in his ear. Or to the rest of the Ghaal around the lab, where they watched with equal gleams in their eyes. Some of them stared at Eldich and others at my spread legs. Involuntarily, my thighs twitched as I tried to close my legs, and another sob raked through my body when I couldn't move.

"You can smell her, can't you? You can smell her sweet sex."

Eldich grumbled something that ended in a growl, and I gasped as the Ghaal laughed and pointed when the cloth covering Eldich's crotch shifted as his cock twitched.

"I'd touch her, but I think that would only make the scent of her fear override her cunt. So, I won't push any tools inside her and force her to orgasm... yet."

My legs jerked again as I tried to close them, and with another whimper, I squeezed my eyes shut for a moment before forcing them to open and returning my gaze to Eldich.

There was another Ghaal who stood next to me, and he twirled something in his hand. When the Ghaal behind Eldich nodded at him, he gripped my hair in his fist and yanked my head backward. I stared into the orange-ringed eyes of one of my captors, and the sickly smell of his skin washed over me as I was unable to drag my gaze from the ring of color around his pupils.

He made a quick slice with the blade down my cheek, and I cried out. He tugged my hair as I tried to jerk away from him, and I bit my lip and tried to stop the sounds of my whimpers from escaping. There was a jumble of sounds as Eldich yanked against his restraints, and he snarled as the Ghaal repeated the action on my other cheek.

"All you're doing by hurting her is making me desire to kill you," Eldich growled out.

The Ghaal let my hair go. I dropped my chin to my chest and breathed against the stinging pain in my cheeks.

"He's right, Rah."

"So…" Rah, the Ghaal behind Eldich, said as he held his hand out. "Give me the knife."

The weapon exchanged hands, and before I could react, the Ghaal's hands were on either side of my face, and I was forced to look at Eldich. "Watch," he whispered in my ear. Automatically, I closed my eyes, displaying the only form of rebellion I could. I opened them when my cheeks were squeezed hard, and he growled out, "Watch your *mate.*"

Rah leaned forward and sliced a long, deep cut across Eldich's chest. A stream of gray blood oozed from the wound as Eldich's back arched against the pain, but he didn't make a sound. Rah continued cutting and slicing along Eldich's torso and arms before moving down and doing the same to his thighs. The beautiful tone of his sandy skin was soon slick with the grayish blood, which thinned and smeared as the Ghaal moved his hand rapidly from one place to another. Eldich's chest was heaving, and his eyes rolled in his head before they landed on Rah as animalistic snarls and growls emanated from him.

This was the animal they wanted him to become.

Eldich's pupils were blown wide, and the snarling didn't stop, even when he looked at me.

"Let the animal to the surface, Synth, until you're nothing but instinct."

Eldich roared as the blade was plunged into his thigh, and I screamed. "*No!*"

"Rah, this can't work. We need to stimulate *her.*"

"It'll work," Rah responded to the Ghaal behind me as he grabbed a handful of Eldich's hair, pulled back, and forced Eldich to stare into his eyes. "We'll make him animal again, then chuck him in a cell with the female." I gasped and tried to pull away from the Ghaal holding me as Rah chuckled. "He won't want to hurt her, but he'll have to take out his rage another way."

CHAPTER

II

ELDICH

Although, in the past, I had endured less pain at the hands of the Ghaal than Lanir had, I was no stranger to torture. Rah was relentless with his attacks, and every nerve in my body was on fire as he cut and sliced into my skin. Many were fine cuts that barely broke the skin, but as he criss-crossed them over each other, my nerves screamed in response. With each new cut, I snarled at him, and another string attached to my self-control severed.

After hours, I could barely focus on Amy's face as she cried while I roared and lashed out at the Ghaal. Rah stopped as abruptly as he started, and with a huff, he splashed antiseptic over my skin to save me from infection. They wouldn't want their *tool* to be unusable, but it added to the sting of my wounds, and I roared again.

They threw Amy and me into a cell together, although it took six of them to move and restrain me, and then left us alone.

The Ghaal knew if I could see them, I would go for *them* and not *her*.

Amy crouched in the far corner of the cell, and her hands partially covered her face as she watched me pace the length of the floor. I tried to keep my thoughts clear, but the longer I raged, the more the lingering pain continued to sting, and with every breath, I could smell my blood and her skin, then the less of me there was inside.

The more animal I became.

Amy's scent carried the heavy odor of fear, and once I picked up on it, it was all I could think of.

I must *keep her safe.*

I stopped my pacing and turned my head slowly toward Amy. Her fear spiked when I moved toward her. I stilled, tilted my head to the side, and studied her as I approached. Beautiful female. She shouldn't be curled up in the corner of a cell—she should be under me receiving pleasure.

Becoming pregnant with my child.

My nostrils flared as I breathed in deeply and captured every essence of her in the air between us.

Fear drowned out most everything else, and I frowned as I paused, inches from touching her.

Why is she afraid of me?

She is to be my mate.

"Eldich…" Amy whispered as I took another step toward her.

She needn't be afraid of me. We belonged together.

Amy moved her hands so her palms were flat against the cell wall behind her and braced herself to move away from me as her eyes darted to my crotch. "Eldich. Please don't do this."

She smelled so… *female.* Beyond the fear was her scent, and it was intoxicating. I needed more, to be surrounded by her scent as my cock was surrounded by the warmth of her cunt. Images of her under me took over my mind until I had to blink through them to see her in front of me. The images blurred, and my fingers twitched as I imagined the feel of her naked skin under my hands. I looked down and noticed for the first time my cock was hard and as aching for her as I was. While my skin still burned and tingled where I had been cut, it hardly mattered anymore. I could ignore the discomfort because before me was my *mate,* and her body called to mine.

She was scared, but she'd be happy once my cock was inside her. I'd have her screaming with pleasure.

I couldn't help the growl that escaped my throat at the thought. I threw my head back, reached down, and palmed my cock through my loin cloth.

Loin cloth? No. *Too much.*

With a snarl, I ripped the fabric away, and Amy screamed at the action.

Is she impressed by my cock? I grinned.

When my eyes met hers, her bottom lip trembled.

"Eldich..." she said my name again, and I never thought my name could sound so sweet as it did when it came from her lips. She squealed as I approached, and I closed the gap between us as she scrambled into a standing position. Her back hit the cell wall as I caged her in between my arms and leaned in to inhale her scent.

Amy's hair fluttered around her shoulders as I released a heavy breath, and I grabbed a handful of it and twisted it around my fingers, bringing it to my nose to inhale again. The rumbling growl in my chest started again and grew impossibly loud when Amy placed her hands on my chest. Her soft fingers against my wounds made me hiss, but beyond that, the knowledge that she was *touching* me had my hips thrusting against her.

"Please don't do this." Amy's bottom lip trembled again, and I ran my thumb across it as she whimpered. "I know you don't want to hurt me."

Hurt her?

I would never hurt my mate.

To show her this, I wrapped an arm around her waist and tugged her next to me. She gasped, and her fingers curled against my chest. I pressed my lips to her neck and ran my tongue along her collarbone. Amy's gasp morphed into a moan, and I ground my cock against her. The fabric of the loose tunic she wore was too much between us, and I scrambled at it, trying to tear it from her body.

I needed her skin.

I needed her naked against me.

Amy's hands came down and grabbed her clothing. She tried to hold it in place, but I tugged at it to lift it over her head.

"I would never hurt you," I growled the words out, the sound harsh against my ears. I shook my head and tried again, but the growl remained. "Never hurt you."

"Eldich, please… not like this."

Something stabbed at the back of my mind, telling me this was wrong. But she was *Amy,* and she was *mine.* She wanted me. I could smell it on her, and my pheromones released and flooded the space between us, eliciting a gasp from her.

My shoulders jerked as I tried to stop myself from going further.

No, something is wrong.

She's afraid.

My mate is afraid of me.

This is what the Ghaal wanted.

"Not like this, please. It'll hurt like this."

My entire body shuddered at her words, and with her still caged against the wall between my arms, I started to tremble as I desperately tried to cling to any control I had remaining. I damned the DNA that made me this way and the Ghaal who had used me. I was playing right into their hands, doing exactly as they predicted I would.

But I wouldn't hurt Amy. Not ever.

But my hips still moved against her as I sought friction against my cock.

I couldn't stop.

"Hurt me," I whispered and gritted my teeth as a wave of her sweet scent came across me when she looked up at me.

"What?"

"Hurt me, please. Snap me out of this."

Amy shook her head. She didn't want to hurt me. *She wants me.*

I leaned in to lick her neck again, and when my tongue touched the salty tang of her skin, I was rewarded with a sharp pain between my legs. I howled, reared back, and cupped my hands over my sack.

Amy rushed forward with her hands outstretched. "Oh my God, I'm so *sorry.* You told me to hurt you, right? Oh God, it wasn't just some kinky talk, was it?"

I held up a hand to stop her words, rested my other palm on my knee, and took a few deep breaths. What I needed was fresh air that wasn't infused with her feminine scent, but we were locked in a cell with no windows, and she was all around me. Amy had done as I asked, acting on instinct when I didn't back away as I should have and brought her knee to my groin. The pain was immediate and sharp, and it was enough to shock me from my state.

Instinct no longer controlled my mind, but now conflicting thoughts fought within me.

Without looking up, I whispered, "Can you ever forgive me?"

"Oh, Eldich…" The relief in her voice sent another pang of guilt to my chest, and I resisted the urge to shrug her hand away when she placed it on my shoulder. Her thumb traced small circles on my skin, and the sensation was relaxing and stimulating.

I should tell her to stop.

But I wasn't strong enough.

I *wanted* her to touch me.

"It's not your fault," she said, and when I didn't respond, she bent down, twisting around so her face was underneath mine, and I was forced to look at her. "Misha explained about your instincts, and that is exactly what the Ghaal is trying to exploit." When my expression twisted, she reached out and placed her hand over mine on my knee. "But you fought it. You were strong, and you fought it. I knew you wouldn't hurt me."

"You're not safe with me," I muttered, straightened, and stepped back from her. "It should never have got as far as it did."

"I forgive you." But she looked at the floor and rubbed her upper arm with her hand.

I squeezed my eyes shut. "I wasn't strong enough." Sinking to the floor, I leaned against the wall and ran my hands down my face. "Tomorrow, when they realize we haven't mated, they'll try again. They'll keep trying until I can't fight it anymore."

Amy's lips were pressed together in a fine line. "Couldn't we just... *tell* them we did it?"

My eyes found hers. "They'd examine you to check."

Amy's legs clenched together, and she bit her bottom lip. After a moment's hesitation, she walked toward me and sat beside me, her small arm brushing against mine. I didn't have the willpower to move away—the contact was too much for me to resist. It was all I could allow myself to have.

"How are your cuts?" She pursed her lips as she looked over my arms and chest. "They look so painful."

"It doesn't matter."

Amy's brow furrowed, but she said nothing for a

moment. I used the pause to take a few more deep breaths, hoping I could control myself fully again.

And frightened I couldn't.

"Maybe we should have sex," Amy said.

I was certain I must have misheard, and my eyes shot to Amy to find her staring up at me earnestly. Her gaze fell to my lap, where my cock was starting to harden again, and I shifted my legs. Her expression morphed from uncertainty into something pained when I said nothing, and I cursed myself for hurting her.

"Amy," I waited until she looked back into my eyes before I continued, "I would love nothing more than to fuck you." Her cheeks turned pink, but she held my gaze. "But not like this. I want you to come to me when you want me, not when you're forced to."

"You're not forcing me. You stopped."

"I'm not forcing you, but *they* are through circumstance. We just have to be strong. The others will come for us."

Amy's lip trembled again, and when I managed to pull my gaze from her beautiful lips, I saw the tears forming in her eyes. "Can I ask you…" she sniffed, then released a frustrated groan before she wiped her face angrily. "So sick of crying," she muttered. But the tears didn't stop, and she simply ignored them as she looked up at me. "Can I ask you an incredibly selfish question?"

"Anything." I watched her cautiously.

"Why didn't you... the Synths, I mean... why didn't you come for us when we were first taken? We were all alone." Her voice broke with the control she'd been holding on to, and Amy hid her face in her hands and brought her knees to her chest as her shoulders shook with her sobs.

I thought my chest couldn't hurt anymore and that the chasm around my heart couldn't open any wider, but her words and the pain in her voice brought down a weight upon me that crushed me completely. "I would have, Amy. Please believe I would have come for you." I cast my memory back to all those years ago—Amy and her friends were taken before the Ghaal were cut off from intergalactic trade. It was what they *did* to Amy and the other females that got the Ghaal cut off in the first place. The Ghaal had been purchasing abducted species before the humans, but it wasn't until the humans that it was discovered what they had been doing, the cruelty they'd been doing it with, and to what extent they were going to ensure impregnation. Taking species from certain unprotected planets wasn't illegal in small numbers, and even using them for DNA-related research was allowed so long as they weren't harmed. But the Ghaal—as they often did—went too far and were cut off. A red shield was cast around the planet. They then had to seek out the help of the Moeks—essentially pirates, who would do questionable things in exchange for supplies and the abundant fuel here, while they, too, searched for the answer to their dying species. It took years for the Ghaal to get more humans, and they tried every species they could get their hands on in between.

Then Misha and her friends were taken, but unlike Amy, because the Moeks couldn't land, they couldn't be brought directly to the Ghaal and were dropped from a distance in the units where my brothers found them.

"We didn't know until it was too late," I whispered, and unable to stop myself from touching Amy, I wrapped an arm around her and tugged her next to me. It wasn't enough, and I pulled her onto my lap. I needed her as close as she could be and to wrap my arms around her so I could make her feel as safe as possible, even in this cell. She didn't protest but simply tucked her head against my chest and sobbed quietly. I bit back the hiss as her cheek brushed my wounds. "When you were taken, we didn't know what they were doing. I'm so sorry."

Ilk explained he'd suspected they had the first lot of human females for a while, months perhaps, as they were taken before the planet was cut off from trade. Some were killed before the cutoff, others after. Their deaths were spread out. Some were perhaps accidental and occurred during the attempts to impregnate them, and some were likely killed after impregnation in a hasty and desperate need to *confirm.*

It was when my brothers and I saw the units falling that we knew we had to act. We had gathered together and made plans to steer any and all species away from the Ghaal colony. Unable to return ourselves, we did everything we could from a distance.

After the death of the first lot of humans, the Ghaal must have taken anything the Moeks could get to them. But evidently, they were always waiting for more humans.

How long was Amy at their mercy? Weeks? Months? How many experiments did they do? How invasive were they?

The full impact of what Amy must have suffered through hit me—how could I not have seen it before? I'd been swept up in the journey of the latest humans abducted, most of whom had managed to escape the grips of the Ghaal with my brothers' help. Even when I was told of Amy and Tegan, I didn't consider the horrors they had experienced.

Where were we the entire time? It was after our escape, and we were still trying to figure out where we fit in the world.

Amy and Tegan suffered long with no one to save them.

So why should Amy believe she was going to be saved this time?

"It's different this time, Amy, I promise you. We'll get you out, and the Ghaal will never be able to hurt you again."

She lifted her face from my chest, her cheeks blotchy with emotion and smeared with my blood. "I don't understand why we can't just escape now. You said you could bend the bars in the window in the cell Misha and Tegan are in, so why can't your brothers just break them free?"

"Because the Ghaal will keep coming. Don't you see? Look at what happened to Misha. Sahcor did just that and broke her out, but the Ghaal didn't stop coming after her. They captured and released her again and again and used her as bait before ultimately bringing her back in. They'll *never* stop."

"So, we're alone again, *hoping* someone will come and save us."

"You're not alone." I brushed my fingers through her hair, a satisfied growl rumbling through my chest when she didn't flinch or pull away from my touch but rested her cheek against my shoulder. "This time, you have me."

CHAPTER 12

AMY

How long had it been since I felt *safe?*

I couldn't even remember.

Definitely not since being taken from Earth.

But straddling Eldich's lap with his large arms wrapped around me and my ear pressed to his chest, I felt protected. A low growl was rumbling through his chest, and it was a constant hum against me, almost enough to drown out the gentle thud of his heartbeat. It was near impossible to keep my thoughts from Misha and Sahcor—her alien boyfriend—and the connection they seemed to share. Not to mention the fact that she was pregnant with his child, and outside of our current circumstances, she seemed happy about that.

I think she must love him.

I debated asking Eldich his thoughts on the pregnancy, but Misha hadn't even gotten a chance to tell Sahcor yet, and it wasn't my place to give her news away.

When she told Sahcor, I wanted it to be a happy moment for them, not desperate words exchanged between bars.

My tears slowed and eventually stopped, and I relaxed in Eldich's embrace. While I could feel his cock between us, hard and insistent, Eldich wasn't moving his hips at all and seemed to be ignoring it. I was trying to ignore it, too, but every now and then, it would twitch. He'd torn off his loin cloth in his rage earlier, and I had no underwear, so the smooth skin of his cock rested against my exposed pussy.

And damn, if I wasn't tempted to rub against him.

He was right, of course. If we were going to have sex, this wasn't the right time or place. It would be mechanical and ever-present in both our minds that it was exactly what the Ghaal wanted. We were prisoners here—experiments even. What would happen if I did get pregnant? I squeezed my eyes closed. *No.* Eldich was right. When we came together, it would be when we were free.

When I sat up straight, Eldich's arms loosened

around me to allow me to come face-to-face with him, but he continued touching me and kept his large hands on my lower back. It was nice—being so small compared to him. I didn't want to have my thoughts directed to my physical appearance—it seemed a shallow consideration to have, given the circumstances, but I couldn't help it. When you grow up with it being constantly brought to your attention, with people telling you to diet—even if they're trying their best to suggest it in a friendly way—or not-so-subtly commenting on what you eat, it becomes something always living in your mind. So, if someone else wasn't pointing out I wasn't skinny, then I would be pointing it out to myself. From the horrible nicknames in school to the emotional manipulation of past boyfriends, my weight was never far from the forefront of my mind.

I huffed out a humorless laugh. Even in this incredibly messed-up situation—captured by aliens and snuggling with a different alien—I was *still* thinking about it. Funny how much people's words can stick with us.

But Eldich was *huge.* Seven feet, maybe? And his hands... *his hands...* they made me feel simply tiny in comparison. He'd seen me and never stopped looking at me since, as though I was the most beautiful thing he'd ever seen. It was hard not to be flattered by that.

When I focused on his face, Eldich watched me intently.

"May I touch you?" I blurted out. His eyebrows shot up, and I felt my cheeks flame again. "I mean… nothing too intense. I just want to… touch you."

I was doing a terrible job at explaining to Eldich *why* I wanted to touch him, but he didn't seem offended by my poor reasoning of *wanting to touch him because I wanted to touch him,* and he wasn't looking at me like I was a weirdo.

Quite the opposite, in fact—his cock twitched again between us, and his pupils blew out slightly at my words.

There were so many reasons I wanted to touch him—comfort being one. He was an alien, after all, and another part of it was simply wanting to know what his skin felt like, to explore his body slightly, because in some ways we were so similar but others so vastly different. I also liked how he wanted me—outside of the Ghaal involvement—and maybe I just wanted to forget everything outside this damn cell and simply have a moment with him. As though this was a private moment between us—a man and a woman attracted to each other, in those early moments of discovering what the other one's body felt like.

I didn't know how to begin explaining this, but apparently, I didn't need to explain it.

Eldich nodded and said, "Of course, you can

touch me."

Steeling myself, I tried to hide the nerves that immediately flared in my stomach and created a whirlwind of butterflies as I lifted my hands to his chest. *Can he tell I'm nervous?* My heart must be beating so hard, and surely, he could hear it. Eldich's eyes never left my face, and every time my gaze would flick back to his, I'd find him looking at me intently, his expression unreadable.

The texture of his skin was wonderful, and I ran my fingers over his chest—careful to avoid the wounds—and up over his shoulders. He felt like smooth rock, not artificially smooth, but just enough texture he felt as though he could be part of his environment, like the finest sand.

I'd never experienced anything like it.

When I moved my palms down his arm, Eldich obediently lifted his hand so I could explore further. I touched each of his four fingers in turn, each long and thick.

"For the trees," he muttered, and I met his gaze.

"Sorry?"

"My hands adapted to be larger and more dexterous to assist with climbing and manipulating the trees from the woodlands I live in."

It took me a moment to register. "Because you're adaptive, I remember. Misha said."

"My feet, too," he said, and I remained straddling him but turned to look at his feet. His toes definitely appeared longer than I would have suspected they'd be in proportion to the rest of him, and when he wiggled them, there was a lot of movement there. I could absolutely imagine them curling around a branch and pictured him jumping between giant trees like Tarzan. "Do they disgust you?" he asked when I continued to stare.

I shook my head and smiled as I turned back to face him. "No. I'm just curious." I traced up his arms with both hands. "And these?" I asked. His skin was a deep, sandy yellow, but there were white vertical streaks up his body like someone had stamped him with paint.

"Camouflage between the trunks."

"Of course. You told me before..." My cheeks heated as I glanced away from Eldich's intense stare as I tried to hide any awkwardness.

This was a very strange situation.

"What is the purpose of these?" Eldich lifted his hands and grabbed both my earlobes between his fingers. When I stuttered through a response that never turned into a sentence, he started to rub gently.

Lord. I closed my eyes. *Why is this so sensual?*

"Um..." I whispered, my breath caught as he kept rubbing. I'd never thought of ears as erotic, but *damn.* "My ears..."

Eldich laughed, a deeper rumble of a sound than I was expecting. I blinked rapidly. He smelled *amazing*—earthly, musky, and like *sex.* "I meant the holes. These aren't natural."

"Oh… *oh!*" I said as realization hit. Damn, he was getting into my head. It seemed I couldn't think straight around this man… this *alien.* I was weirdly attracted to him before when it was just him and me awake, and he'd cupped my cheek as he reached between the bars. But the more time has gone on, although it hasn't been *long,* the less my attraction to him seemed *weird.*

Because why not, right? Misha had paired up with Sahcor, and perhaps the other human girls who were abducted with Misha had done the same.

"Those are where I had my ears pierced." Eldich stared at me blankly, so I explained, "Some people get piercings in their body, and they'll wear pieces of jewelry in them."

His eyes narrowed slightly, and I giggled quietly. Evidently, he thought this practice was strange but was too polite to say so. "You can say it's weird if you think it's weird," I said and grabbed his wrists. I needed him to stop touching me like that. It was distracting. "I won't be offended."

"I'm sure there are many customs that differ between our species."

I giggled again. "Such a tactful response. A very polite way of saying *it's weird. Your species is weird.*"

He chuckled again, and I released his wrists before he moved his hands down and settled them on my shoulders. But his touch was only still for a moment, and then his thumbs started rubbing gently against my collarbones while his fingers kneaded my shoulders.

"I thought I was supposed to be touching you," I whispered as I closed my eyes and relaxed into his touch.

"We can touch each other."

There he was again, using that sexy voice. That deep tone penetrated right into my body and made my ovaries scream *make a baby with this man!*

Alien. Make a baby with this *alien.*

My eyes shot open. "Eldich..." he stopped rubbing at my tone, and his brow furrowed. "Why do I want you so badly right now? I mean, I was attracted to you earlier, but with you touching me like this, even though we're in this cell, it doesn't make sense. I should be scared, but all I can think about is having sex with you."

His eyes closed for a moment as his grip on my shoulders tightened, and a shudder ran down his spine before he regained himself. "Pheromones," he said and opened his bright green eyes to stare into mine. "I release them when I'm attracted to someone. It's not something I can stop, and I'm sorry."

"Are they drugging me?"

"No. Never. They simply increase arousal, enhancing any existing attraction."

"Oh." My cheeks flamed again. *When did I become this giggling, blushing girl?* "That makes sense."

"I can make you come. You might feel better."

It was my turn to shudder. He'd said it so matter-of-factly, but there was a darkening of his expression and a slight shift of his tone. For a moment, I thought he'd *growled* at me, but it was that rumble in his chest, and damn, if that wasn't sexy as hell. Those simple words sent images through my mind of all the things I wanted to do to his body and wanted him to do with mine. The way he looked at me as if I was nothing short of a goddess, I wanted that while he looked down at me as I lay underneath him.

My body reacted to thoughts I couldn't control, and I simply couldn't help the jerk of my hips. The movement shifted his cock so it slid between my pussy lips and over my clit. Eldich groaned, and the growl in his chest doubled in volume. His nostrils flared as his hands moved down to cup my ass. "You smell so good, Amy."

"You can *smell* me? Oh my God."

How long has it been since I've been able to bathe properly?

On instinct, I tried to close my legs, and my thighs tightened around where I straddled him. But Eldich kept his grip on me and pulled me forward again, causing that delicious drag over my clit and my breasts to push against the hardness of his chest.

When I moaned, he did too.

"Don't be embarrassed. Your cunt smells *incredible,*" he whispered the words into my ear, and I just about came on the spot. "I haven't penetrated you, yet you moan like *that...*" he punctuated the word with another drag of my hips forward, and I shuddered again. "Why? Tell me why you make such delicious sounds, Amy, because I want to hear more of them."

"I thought... we shouldn't... you didn't want to..."

"I want everything with you, but I won't sink into you the way I desire. Not here. But I can make you come. You're trembling on top of me, and I want to pleasure you. So, tell me why this..." he gripped my hips and jolted me forward against his cock again, and I groaned, "... makes you make sounds like that."

"M-my clit..." I stuttered, clinging to his shoulders when I was barely holding onto my sanity. I was trying desperately not to overthink this. "My clitoris. It's like... a little bundle of nerves. It'll make me come if stimulated." The half smile I had at the oddness of explaining this so clinically was wiped from my face when Eldich jolted his hips, and the bump of the head of his cock hit my clit. "Fuck!" I cried out.

He kept going and held my hips still so he could thrust his cock between my lips. I was so wet his cock slid easily over my clit, and each movement pushed me closer toward the edge. Eldich closed his eyes and tilted his head back against the wall as he thrust hard against me.

"I can't wait to fuck you, Amy," he muttered, his eyes still closed. "Just sink my cock into your wet cunt and feel you around me."

"Me too," I admitted. There was no point in denying it—I wanted Eldich as much as he wanted me, perhaps more. I'd lost my ability to concentrate as my climax drew closer. The slightest tilt of my hips, and he'd sink inside me. But he was right—not here, not now. "Eldich," I gasped out, and my fingers dug into his shoulders. "Don't stop… I'm going to…"

"Come on my cock, Amy."

Fuck! That *voice.*

I came and shuddered on Eldich's lap as he continued to thrust me through my orgasm. He groaned loudly, and the sound echoed around the cell as a rush of warmth splashed between us. I looked down as another stream of clear cum spurted from his cock as he came on his stomach and over my thighs.

Eldich's head fell back against the wall, and I slumped against his chest.

His large arms wrapped around me and held me close.

For the first time since being on this planet, I fell asleep feeling safe.

CHAPTER 13

ELDICH

Amy slept, and I held her throughout the night.

There were no windows in this cell and no way to tell when daylight was approaching. But I was certain whenever it did, the Ghaal would come too. They'd pick up on the scent of sex in the air from Amy's and my cum and get excited. I snarled and wrapped my arms tighter around Amy as she slept and pulled her protectively against my chest as if I could stop the inevitable simply by holding her.

There was no good ending to this night.

If the Ghaal thought we had sex, they would want to check if Amy was pregnant. If they found out we didn't, then the torture would recommence.

I would take any pain I needed to protect Amy, but last time, I had been closer to losing control than I thought I would. The lines between instinct and rational thinking had been blurred, and my body overtook my mind after only one day.

One day.

How much longer could I keep it up?

What if I got to a point where even Amy inflicting pain on me no longer brought me under control?

I'd never hurt her, but we were created by the Ghaal for a purpose.

Perhaps I was destined to lose control.

The door in the hall slid open, and the noise was enough to jerk Amy from her sleep. She began whimpering when the Ghaal approached, and I tucked her against me and glared at the Ghaal as they came level with the cell and peered between the bars.

"Can you smell it?" one said.

The other lifted his head and sniffed the air before a sickly grin spread across his face. "Did you fuck her?"

I was thankful they spoke in our native language so Amy wouldn't be exposed to the crudeness of their remarks. Although I suspected she would know what they were asking. I didn't answer and continued to glare at them. His grin vanished. He hovered his hand over the silver ball and unlocked the cell. Immediately, I scrambled to my feet and helped Amy to hers before I shuffled her behind me and backed up, hiding her in the corner. I knew it would do no good, but it went against everything in my core not to at least *try* to protect her.

Both the Ghaal took in my naked body and the spill of my seed on my stomach before there was angry muttering between them. "If he fucked her, he didn't deposit inside her."

In unison, they drew their weapons, one with a longer stick which could be used to deliver painful shocks, the other with the small wand specifically designed to kill me.

"Move," he barked out the order.

"Amy," I whispered and turned my head slightly. "We have to go back to the lab."

"I don't want to." Amy whimpered again.

"I know, but we have to. This will be over soon."

She trembled as I stepped forward, and she followed me, clinging to my arm as I held it behind my back.

"Don't touch her," I hissed at the Ghaal as they moved toward us, and they shared knowing smiles. But they backed up despite still holding their weapons out toward us. With Amy staying behind me, we returned to the lab. The Ghaal pointed at the chairs we were bound to yesterday, and Amy trembled again and tucked herself in further behind me.

"No," I spoke to the Ghaal. "Not this time."

"You don't have a choice, Synth."

"I want to talk, to make an alternative plan."

"You had your chance," one hissed out, brandishing the weapon. "You could've fucked her last night, and you didn't. Now into the chair, or I'll kill you, and in the minutes it takes you to die, I'll fuck her in front of you and show you how it's done."

The growl started in my chest, and Amy released a squeak of fright as I snarled but shuffled in closer against me. "Let me remind you, torturing her does nothing but anger me. You almost got your result yesterday by torturing me."

The Ghaal watched me warily for a moment before his gaze dipped again to where my cum had dried against my skin. He said nothing but indicated the chair with another point of his finger. With gentle coaxing, I got Amy to sit, hating myself every second, before I sat opposite her as we had done the day before. Only this time, we allowed ourselves to be restrained without a fight. *This* was the true torture as I watched Amy cry while she was tied up and her legs spread again. The way her eyes widened as she glanced between the line of torture tools being set up and me and sobbed each time our eyes met, shattering me further.

I hated this, but getting myself killed would not help Amy, Misha, or Tegan.

My brothers wouldn't let this go on. They would've suspected what happened when I didn't return from hunting, and they would come for us.

The Ghaal was patient and would wait for all six females.

But they wouldn't get them.

AMY

For a full day, they tortured Eldich in front of me, and I don't think I've ever cried so hard in my life. Whenever I thought I had control over my tears, they'd poke him again with that cattle-prod thing, and he would arch against the chair with his teeth gritted against the pain.

No matter how much I screamed at them to stop, they kept going.

The only break was halfway through the day to give me food and water and allow me precious moments to relieve myself. The Ghaal tried to offer food to Eldich as well, but he wasn't interested. After the half day of torture, his eyes rolled wildly in his head, and he seemed unable to focus on anything. Once I'd choked down the rubbery strips of food and was restrained again, I leaned forward as far as I could in my chair.

"Eldich?" I whispered.

Once again, there was no point in whispering,

not really. The Ghaal was close, and they all paused in their movements to see what his reaction would be to me talking. Eldich's eyes continued to roll, and the green of his irises was small around his enlarged pupils. As I opened my mouth to speak again, his gaze finally rested on me and steadied.

"That's it. It's me. Everything is going to be okay." I couldn't keep the tremble from my voice, feeling like I was lying to him. Misha and Eldich both seemed filled with such certainty the other Synths would be coming to rescue us and yet I still had to sit here and watch them torture him.

And no one came.

Eldich said nothing, and my words were rewarded only with an angry snort of air through his nose.

"Eldich…" This time, at the sound of my voice, he lunged forward, or at least attempted to, but the strong binds held him in the chair. The Ghaal had learned from yesterday when Eldich had managed to almost break free and gone were the ropes made from some artificial material. Now, the binds were thick metal, controlled with the same type of silver ball that was outside the cells and responded to the Ghaal's touch. I recoiled as Eldich's chair shuddered and creaked, and when he found he couldn't get closer to me, the wild look returned to his eyes, and he only struggled harder.

The Ghaal spent the rest of the afternoon

alternating between shocking and taunting Eldich by lifting the fabric that covered my pussy and goading him with cruel words.

At last, they put down the prod.

One of the Ghaal eyed Eldich, who was now trying to lunge toward me every few seconds. It was nearly impossible not to be afraid. Those arms I had felt so safe in last night were awfully strong, and the cords of his muscles were taut with tension.

In this state, he could easily hurt me accidentally.

"How do we get him to the cell? The second we release the binds—"

"Take her. Throw her in their cell. Then clear the area. He'll follow."

Eldich roared as I was released and dragged away. "Shh... shh..." I tried to comfort him through tears as I was grabbed under my arms and heaved to my feet. "Stay calm, Eldich. It's okay." His chair creaked with every movement now, and the Ghaal chattered excitedly amongst themselves as I was dragged to the cell. They shoved me in, leaving the doors and gate open between where Eldich was and where I now stood, pressed against the rear of the cell.

"Release him!" one called after they hid and secured themselves.

From the lab, I could hear Eldich's roar, louder and more gravelly than before. A burst of surprised shouting followed by a sickening squeal and crunch made me cover my ears with my hands and cringe.

Eldich appeared in the doorway, framed by the light behind him. His chest heaved as his eyes fell on the Ghaal ducked down near the cell's entry. He stared at them for a beat that seemed to linger in the air, but then his gaze found me, and there was no more hesitation. Eldich rushed into the cell, ignoring the door as it was slammed behind him and locked, trapping us again.

"Eldich, *wait!*" I cried out.

But he was on me, and the Ghaal laughed as Eldich pinned me to the floor. They waited by the cell, watching him, but every time Eldich would look up and see them there, he would stop moving and snarl at them.

The Ghaal simply laughed again before leaving us alone.

CHAPTER 14

AMY

Eldich's weight on top of me was intense, and his forearms were at either side of my head as his hips thrust on an instinct I knew he couldn't control.

"Eldich…" I was unable to close my legs as his thick torso was between them, a solid mass of muscle I had no chance of moving. Gripping his face, I tried to force him to look at me. "*Eldich!*" But his eyes were unfocused, his pupils so wide it gave his eyes the illusion of being all black, with only the thinnest ring of green visible. I didn't want to hurt him, but I knew he wouldn't want to be like this either. When he'd rushed me into the cell, I'd screamed purely in reaction, but it took me only a few seconds of searching inside myself to realize I *wasn't* afraid of him.

Afraid of how he could accidentally hurt me. *Absolutely.*

But scared of Eldich himself? *No.*

When I slapped him across the cheek, he snarled. Then his lip lifted into almost a smirk, and he bared his slightly sharp teeth, leaned his face down to the crook of my neck and shoulder, and licked my skin with a long drag of his tongue. The feel of his textured tongue over me made me moan involuntarily, and Eldich groaned in response and inhaled deeply against my neck and hair.

I picked up on his scent again—the pheromones he'd told me about releasing as he tried to seduce me.

Against his will.

Eldich wouldn't want this.

As the length of his cock rubbed against the inside of my thigh, I had a moment of internal debate.

Should I simply let this happen?

They were going to keep torturing Eldich if we didn't. If I submitted to him, he had less chance of hurting me in this wild frenzy he was in than if I resisted.

Amy, I would love nothing more than to fuck you. But not like this. When his voice echoed in my mind,

I squeezed my eyes shut.

He didn't want this, and none of this was his fault.

I couldn't knee him in the nuts again, not from this angle. Perhaps if I...

Reaching between us, I wrapped my hand around one of his balls and squeezed. If I did it hard enough, maybe he'd back off and snap back to normal. Eldich groaned loudly, and the growling started in his chest as he thrust harder against my leg.

He likes it.

Okay, plan B.

I wrapped my hand around his cock, and Eldich shuddered with pleasure and thrust against my palm. I squeezed his shaft tightly and let him fuck my hand. "That's it..." I whispered, rubbing his arm with my other palm. "Come for me, Eldich."

Finally, his eyes found mine, and for a second, I could have sworn clarity returned. But it was gone as quickly as I'd imagined it, and his thrusting picked up pace. I gripped his cock harder, twisting my wrist and working my hand in time with the movement of his hips. Eldich would hate himself for this, and I bit my bottom lip against the rise of emotions. I knew he'd blame himself, and I'd have to be there for him when he came down from this madness. I would have to remind him that none of this was his fault, that he was a victim and a prisoner here just like I was.

I didn't blame him, and I didn't want him to blame himself, either.

While the image of a seven-foot alien rushing at me with his erect cock bouncing and dripping with precum was alarming, the second his hands touched me, I remembered who he was beyond this. Because he didn't tackle me to the floor and immediately penetrate me. Eldich's arms had wrapped around me, and even in this mad state when, he lowered me to the floor, there was something graceful in his movements, and he'd protected my head from hitting the hard floor.

He was *aware* of me.

I wasn't simply a piece of meat or a female to be bred.

Eldich was in there somewhere.

With another groan and a final thrust, he came, and his cum spilled over my stomach and legs. I couldn't help it and giggled nervously. There was *so much cum,* and the clear sticky fluid drenched me.

Eldich collapsed on top of me and rested his face against the crook of my neck. His breath was warm, and I sighed, unsure if I should move my hand or keep cupping his still-hard cock. I gave him some minutes to recover and waited until his breathing became steady and the growling from his chest had eased to a dull hum.

"Eldich?" I whispered as I squeezed his shoulder gently.

He grumbled something, and while I could feel his lips moving against my skin, I didn't recognize any words. Was he saying anything at all, or was this his native language? I bit my lip in indecision. *How far do I push him? Do I let him sleep it off?* Being pinned under his weight would make for an uncomfortable evening, but if it helped him return to normal, I was willing to do it.

I cursed inwardly, wishing I'd asked him these questions last night when I had the chance.

Had Misha had to deal with an out-of-control Synth before?

"Amy…"

I stilled as Eldich spoke, his voice a heavy growl again. He said my name, he had *definitely* said my name, but the voice wasn't his. Eldich's hips started moving again, his cum still on my hand creating lube as he thrust again.

"Shh…" I murmured, rubbing his shoulder. "Let me take care of you."

Eldich groaned as I shoved his shoulder, and I released a sigh of relief as he rolled off me and onto his back. Before he could move, I straddled his legs and took his cock with both of my hands, working him hard. "You need to come again?" I crooned.

Eldich just groaned, and his hands curled into fists at his sides as I worked him harder. When his eyes opened, his pupils were still large, but there was something more of *him* in there. He almost looked frightened before his eyes rolled back, and the growling in his chest started again.

"It's okay, baby…" I hummed out and gently flicked my thumb over the bulbous head of his cock. "Let me make you come again."

His hips bucked into my touch. I didn't let up and worked my hands harder to bring him to climax. Eldich was coming back to me. I could see it in his eyes. Maybe another mind-blowing orgasm could bring him back.

Eldich, please don't hate me for this. I'm trying to help.

Bending, I took the head of his cock into my mouth, choking slightly when Eldich roared and thrust up hard past my lips. I hummed sounds of encouragement and swirled my tongue around the head as I worked him with my hands. His climax took longer to build this time, but as it did, Eldich was thrusting wildly, his back arched and head tilted back, snarling and growling.

"Come on, baby…" I whispered, lifting my head just enough to talk to him between licks. "Come for me."

I sucked hard at the tip of his cock, and as he came, Eldich's hand landed on the back of my head, held me in place, and forced me to swallow his cum as it pumped into my mouth and down my throat.

He let me go when I forced myself to sit straight, coughed, and wiped my mouth on the back of my hand. Again, Eldich collapsed, his eyes closed, and his head lolled to the side.

I watched him carefully as his breathing slowly returned to normal.

I dared not move in case I needed to help him again and sat in silence as he calmed.

Eldich's breathing became so gentle, I suspected he'd fallen asleep, and I was about to climb off his legs when he groaned out, "Amy..."

"I'm here," I whispered. I reached forward but hovered my hand just short of touching his chest. Was he calm enough to be touched yet? I didn't want to set off his instincts again. He would already hate himself for what had happened.

When the growling started in his chest again, I tensed and watched his face as his brow furrowed.

Slowly, Eldich's eyes opened, but he didn't look at me. Instead, he stared resolutely at the ceiling. "Get away from me," he muttered.

"I... what?" His words stung, and my hand automatically moved to my chest. Had I done something wrong? I'd only been trying to help.

My stomach dropped as realization dawned.

Oh God, I'd taken advantage of him.

He was in no state to say *yes* or *no*, and I'd touched him anyway.

Covering my mouth with my hands as my

stomach churned, I shuffled off him. "Oh my God, Eldich, I'm so sorry," I said as I scrambled to the other side of the cell. I sobbed once, unable to cover the sound. "Oh God, you must *hate* me. Can you ever forgive me? I was only trying to help."

Eldich sat up, his legs outstretched in front of him. His eyes were on his lap, covered in his cum, and he stared at his now-flaccid cock as it lay limp against his muscular thigh.

"Forgive you?" he asked, his voice quiet.

"I..." Watching him cautiously, I leaned forward on my knees and placed both hands on the cell floor, ready to move to him if he needed me or away if he hated me. "I touched you without your permission. I was just trying to get you to calm down. I swear, I was only trying to help. I'm so sorry. Please, forgive me."

When his gaze found mine, the pang of pain in my chest was so intense I almost recoiled. I don't think I'd ever seen a look of such sadness in someone's eyes. The pain from him was so visceral I felt as though it shimmered in the air between us, and I blinked rapidly when I realized it was the tears fogging my vision.

My heart sank.

He hates me.

"You helped?" he asked, his voice gravelly with emotion.

"I..." I squeezed my eyes shut for a moment,

desperate to stop my lip from trembling. "I used my hands and mouth. I thought it would be better if you came harder. I knew you didn't want to have sex while in that state..." My eyes filled with tears. "Please, believe me, Eldich. I only wanted to help."

"I remember..." He raised a hand to his head as his brows pulled together. "I could see and *feel* you, but I couldn't stop myself." I didn't know what to say, so I simply nodded, giving him time to work through this. When he lifted his gaze to me again, he asked, "You don't hate me?"

I recoiled. "What? *No.* Of *course* not. None of this is your fault." I frowned at him and took an experimental shuffle forward. "Do you hate *me?*"

I gasped as Eldich pushed himself to his feet, closed the gap between us, and scooped me up in one smooth motion. He held me so my legs wrapped around his waist and stepped forward until I was trapped between him and the cell wall.

"Why would I hate you?" he asked. His words were gentle in contrast to the intensity of his stare.

"I touched you while you were in that state." My voice was small and grew quieter at his stare. "I didn't have your permission." Even saying it made my stomach drop and churn.

Eldich said nothing, and I raised my eyes to his again.

"I could've hurt you, I almost..." He shook his head as if to clear the image from his mind.

I cupped his cheek in my hand. "You didn't want to hurt me, I knew that. So, I simply tried to help you come back to *you*, and out of that state they put you in."

"Amy..." The words were a growl again, but this time, when he buried his face against my neck, he nibbled and licked, talking against my skin. "You should hate me for what I almost did, for what I've *done*. But instead, you found a way to help me. I don't deserve you. I'm unworthy to be your mate."

Relief flooded through me, and warmth spread from my heart to my limbs. I held back another sob as emotion welled in my throat. "You don't hate me then?" I couldn't keep the tremble from my voice, but I needed to hear him say it.

"Never. I could *never* hate you." Eldich leaned forward and inhaled the scent of my hair, and his sigh turned into a growl. "I'm thankful to you. I'm thankful *for* you. I need you. I hope you can believe me when I tell you we won't be trapped in here forever."

I nodded as I barely managed to hold back the tears of relief.

But I was also afraid because I still wasn't convinced we'd be rescued and all of this would be over. I'd been here too long, longer than even I had realized. Because beyond the months in captivity, I'd been frozen in time for *years,* and now I was back and a prisoner again. The only difference now was I had Eldich in here with me. And while he made me feel safe and protected, it was all an illusion. Because even with the warmth of his body and hard chest pressed against me, the cold wall of the cell reminded me where I was.

"When we're free, Amy…" Eldich mumbled against my neck, making me squirm and pulling a reluctant giggle from my throat at the tickle of his lips. He pulled me from my musings, although they never truly went away, only pushed to the side. "When we're free, I'm going to feast on your cunt, and then I'm going to fuck you for the rest of our days."

I wanted to believe him, that our rescue was imminent. It's what Eldich believed, but that didn't make it true. I was balancing on a knife's edge of being thankful he was here with me and hating myself for thinking that. His being here with me only meant he, too, was trapped, whereas he should be free with his brothers where he belongs. Sighing, I rested my cheek against his shoulder, unable to stop myself from rolling my hips against him and feeling the length of his cock between my legs.

"I'd like that very much," I whispered, smiling sadly.

"Soon, Amy," he crooned, pushing back against me, the sudden pressure on my clit making me gasp. "Soon."

I wanted to believe him.
I really did.

CHAPTER 15

ELDICH

Amy and I held strained eye contact. For the third day in a row, we were bound to the lab chairs. Twice now, she'd managed to pull me back to myself after my animalistic fits. But as the Ghaal pulled up trays of torture devices next to Amy *and* me, I wasn't convinced she'd be able to do it again. I was already on edge before anything had even happened, my nerves buzzing with adrenaline and anger.

If they torture Amy in front of me while also aggravating me...

I squeezed my eyes shut at that thought.

I'd need to maintain better control.

If I could just direct myself toward the Ghaal instead of Amy.

I knew I'd killed one of them last night, and while it wasn't something I was proud of—I didn't enjoy the feeling of his spine breaking between my hands—I had no regrets.

"I don't know what she's doing," a Ghaal said to me as he inspected his tools. "But we've had enough of these games. At the end of today, she'll be strapped against the cell bars, legs spread and gagged when we unleash you." His smile was cruel, and I snarled at him. "No means for her to talk you down or whatever it is she's doing to keep you from fucking her."

I didn't understand how the Ghaal thought sometimes, but I dared not ask the question looming in my mind lest it give them more ideas.

But the Ghaal spoke anyway, "Rah insists we don't impregnate the females surgically or attempt it ourselves until we have all six." He glanced around at the handful of Ghaal moving about the lab. "I, too, hold our beliefs close. But how much longer must we wait? The females and you being here should be enough bait. I'm a little surprised they haven't come for you yet," he scoffed, lifted a knife, and twirled it in the bright, sterile light. "No matter. We'll send scouts out soon."

Amy watched the Ghaal as he spoke, unable to understand him in our native language. When her eyes found mine, I held her gaze, trying to convey all the reassuring things I wanted to say without words. But would she believe them anyway? Amy had been trapped here before with no one to help or rescue her. To think my future mate had been so close this entire time, and I'd had no idea. The thought sent a stab of pain through my chest as I watched a single tear slide down her cheek.

She was trying so hard to be brave.

I promise you, I thought, wishing she could hear me. *I promise you they'll come for us.*

I stilled as an explosion of sound interrupted my thoughts, and my gaze drifted to the Ghaal, who had been inspecting his tools. He, too, was frozen on the spot, his head tilted as he listened and tried to identify the cause of the sound.

Shouting, running feet, and…

Female voices.

Human voices.

My lip twitched, and I met Amy's gaze, her eyes wide and hopeful as she stared at me. The slightest nod of my head was all she needed, and Amy seemed to sink under the weight of the relief that dropped onto her shoulders.

But her eyes were weary.

She still didn't believe this was over.

I strained my hearing but couldn't find any evidence of my brothers. I worked to keep my expression neutral as Amy watched me closely. The small glimmer of hope in her eyes had waivered when my brows pulled together.

They have come for us.

But where are my brothers?

"Don't fucking *touch* me, you son of a *bitch!*" The female's outburst was met with a chorus of angry muttering from the Ghaal. I looked up as two women strolled into the lab. A circle of Ghaal surrounded them, holding weapons and staying near them but not attacking.

Tori and Erica.

One of the Ghaal shoved Erica forward, and she turned around and glared at him, but as she opened her mouth to speak, they were both ushered toward us.

"Here," a Ghaal snapped.

Tori placed her hands on her hips. "No, this wasn't the deal. We wanted to see *all* our friends." She waved a hand at Amy. "Where are the others?"

A Ghaal hissed at her. "You're in no position to bargain, *female.*"

"I think we are," Erica demanded, matching Tori's pose. "With us here, you're missing only *one* woman until you have all six." She paused as if giving them time to let her words sink in, and when nothing was offered in response, she added, "And only we know where she is."

This was met with immediate chattering until one said in her language, "We don't trust you."

"And *we* don't trust *you.*" Erica's eyes narrowed, and the slightest tremor of her hand betrayed her, and she readjusted it on her hip.

She's scared.

What are they up to?

"Look, it's very simple," Tori said, turning to the Ghaal who had spoken. "We want to be with our friends. We were sick of being separated. This *whole fucking situation* is just *fucked.* I'm sick of running and hiding. I want my *friends.*"

Amy whimpered slightly, her gaze jumping between Tori and me. This wasn't how it was meant to work.

"Don't," she whispered under her breath, the beginning of tears shimmering in her eyes. "Don't do this. Just leave."

Tori's eyes flicked to Amy briefly, but she said nothing.

"The Synths?" A Ghaal inquired.

Erica pressed her lips together. "We left without them knowing. They wanted us to run and hide, but we couldn't leave our friends behind. We just couldn't."

What's going on? Would they *really* leave the safety of my brothers' protection?

"Where is the other female?" a Ghaal snapped.

Erica twisted her hands together. "She wasn't so keen on coming with us. But we know where she is. We hate you, but we still think it's better we're all together. Maybe we can work something out."

Amy shook her head wildly, and I snarled. "What are you *doing?*" Erica turned to me, still twisting her hands together with pain in her eyes. "Get out of here!" I roared, and pulled against the binds in an attempt to startle her. "Get out!"

"I'm sorry," she said and turned her head away from me. "It's the only way we can be together."

"You heard them," the Ghaal hissed to two comrades. "They want to be *together.*"

Tori took a step to the side as a Ghaal approached her. "Touch me, and you'll *never* find the sixth."

With equal sneers, the Ghaal exchanged a look before they turned away, disappeared out the door, and returned moments later with Misha and Tegan. Tegan's eyes were wide and wild, and darted around the room between Amy, me, Tori, Erica, and the Ghaal as she desperately tried to piece it all together.

As was I.

"Where is the sixth female?"

"We'll take you to her." Tori straightened her spine.

"What the hell are you doing?" Misha snapped, fury etched into her features. "I gave up everything to keep you safe!"

The Ghaal stared at Tori and ignored Misha's outburst. "No. You can't be trusted. We won't be led into a trap where the Synths are waiting for us."

Erica and Tori exchanged glances. "You... you have to follow us," Erica said, her voice wavering.

"No," the Ghaal responded, reaching for one of their weapons. "We will not follow you anywhere."

There was a beat of uncomfortable silence that stretched between Erica and Tori as they glanced at each other again. Erica shifted her gaze to the Ghaal who'd spoken and took a slow step backward. As she glanced over her shoulder, she let out a whine when she realized the exit was blocked.

"Run," I shouted.

Erica reached up and curled her fingers into her hair. "They were meant to follow us!" There was a note of hysteria in her voice that sounded unnatural, and I snarled again.

This is their plan?

One last look at each other, and Tori and Erica bolted in opposite directions.

Immediately, they were grabbed by groups of Ghaal and screamed and struggled against them as they were held in place. There was general laughter and muttering as they were subdued by force, their arms and legs held still.

"Surely, you didn't think it would be that easy." Rah came to the forefront and inspected the girls as they glared at him, being held in place by the Ghaal who surrounded them.

"What were you *thinking?*" Misha's voice was

desperate, her face contorted with fear and disbelief. Her attempts to get to Tori and Erica were stalled by a Ghaal holding her. The lab was filling with the Ghaal now—ten, then twenty, all here to watch as the females were restrained by many hands.

"Search them," Rah demanded.

The Ghaal surrounding Erica and Tori began running their hands over their bodies, and the women twisted and kicked out at every chance they got.

"She's armed," one spat out, his hands running up Erica's upper thigh outside the thick pants she wore. With a snarl, he shredded the fabric at the seam, exposing her leg, and pointed to a knife sheath strapped to her thigh.

"This one too." Tori kicked out at the Ghaal as he lifted her dress, giving her thigh a pinch as she released a roar of rage. "Only a knife each? Pathetic. What exactly were you planning?"

Rah barked out a harsh laugh. "Humans are pathetic. Thankfully, we can breed them out of our offspring." Approaching Erica, he ran a finger down her face. She recoiled from his touch and glared at him. "Remember me?" He laughed quietly.

Erica said nothing, but her hands trembled violently. I glanced over as another whimper came from Amy, and when I met her gaze, her eyes were sad.

She wasn't accusing or disappointed. She simply accepted the situation because she never truly believed we would be rescued.

Erica and Tori being caught now was simply another confirmation of the dark reality she'd accepted.

"I think you owe me for last time, female..." Erica started fighting anew when Rah ran his palm over her leg before he reached his fingers into the rip in her pants. "We were going to have some fun with you." The shape of his hand moving under the fabric on her leg pulled a snarl from my lips. This was Ilk's mate, and no one else was to touch her, especially not a Ghaal.

"Leave her *alone,*" I growled out and tugged once again on the restraints on the chair. Rah offered me an amused glance before he shifted his hand and withdrew the knife from the sheath strapped around Erica's thigh. He held it in front of him and ran his fingers up the blade, making clicking noises with his lips and clearly amused by their attempt to arm themselves. The bone knife wasn't big, but it could do some damage if used properly.

But there were only two of them and dozens of Ghaal in the colony.

This was the plan?

My heart hammered in my chest, and my breath quickened. I couldn't believe for a moment Ilk and Vitri would simply allow Erica and Tori to stroll into the Ghaal colony with only knives to defend themselves. Had the women truly left without my brothers' knowledge? They seemed so happy when they were together, the way they'd leaned back against Vitri and Ilk as though they belonged in their arms.

No. This made no sense.

No matter how much they wanted to be with their friends, they wouldn't sneak away from their mates.

Would they?

And if the plan was to lure the Ghaal into a trap? There's no way that could work either. I felt I was going to be sick as the thoughts ran through my mind. Now the Ghaal had five—*five*—of the females, all because of some ill-considered plan?

I needed answers and sought out Tori's eyes with mine. She had frozen on the spot and ignored the chattering and snickering Ghaal, who surrounded her with their hands on her body.

Her gaze was glued firmly to Rah.

What was she waiting for?

He gasped and heaved in a large breath, his eyes wide.

Tori's lip twitched.

Rah made a choking sound as the bone knife clattered to the floor and clutched his wrist.

I froze, my eyes falling to his hand, where the tell-tale deep gray dappling formed on his skin and moved up his arm, a rapid procession of dots of color. It spotted up from where his fingers had touched the blade and made its way to his heart through his veins. My eyes widened as I glanced at Erica to find her looking at me. Her lips were pressed together in a thin line, and she gave an almost unperceivable shake of her head.

There was something in her gaze that made me say nothing nor try to move.

This was the plan.

Rubaee poison.

The room seemed to freeze in time. Rah clutched his chest as the poison made its way into his heart, and the knife skidded across the floor as he stumbled. The Ghaal who surrounded Erica and Tori stared at Rah in disbelief as he fell to his knees, his face contorted in fear and rage. The poison would stop his heart, and there was nothing that could be done—no cure or medicine that would stop the poison from killing him.

Sweat trickled down the back of my neck. This was a risky plan. What was stopping the females from touching the poison by accident? The tainted blades were right there next to their skin.

Rah slumped against the floor.

Dead in seconds.

I glanced at Tori.

Her brows were furrowed, and she rolled her tongue around in her mouth and inside her cheek.

I frowned as my gaze shifted to Erica to find her doing the same.

Seconds later, both women spat mouthfuls of a dark liquid at the Ghaal that surrounded them. At the same time, Tori grabbed the knife from her thigh and swiped at the nearest Ghaal. The ones who were hit by the spray stumbled and could only watch in horror as the poison spread through their bodies before they, too, grabbed at their chests and gasped for air. Anyone who had been nicked by Tori's knife fell, too, and she took advantage of their shock and swiped at more of them. Some of those struck attempted to flee and made it only a handful of steps before they fell.

My jaw dropped.

Poison? In their mouths?

The spell which had kept the Ghaal frozen in place vanished in a moment, and the stunned silence was replaced with angry and panicked shouting. Those who hadn't been hit by the poison fled the lab and shoved each other out of the way in an attempt to make it to the exit first. A small group remained and surrounded Tori and Erica, their hands hovering in front of them in indecision.

With a grin, Erica spat more poison at the nearest ones. Some jumped out of the way while others weren't so fast, and within seconds, they were on their knees.

The remaining few decided it wasn't worth the

risk and fled.

Tori and Erica ran to Amy and began pulling at her restraints, wrapping their fingers around the cold metal and tugging hard as they grunted, desperate to free her.

"The controls!" I shouted and nodded my head at the silver ball near the chair.

"How—" Erica started, but Tori was already heaving a dead Ghaal across the floor as she groaned.

"Help me," she cried out as she gritted her teeth and heaved the Ghaal's body closer. "This fucker is heavy."

Misha seemed to snap into consciousness and ran to help, and the three of them lifted the Ghaal close enough they could hover his hand over the silver ball. Erica's lips twisted in disgust as she released its limp hand and let it fall to the floor before she kicked out at the body and rolled it away from her.

Our restraints released, and before I could stand to help Amy, Erica stopped me, stood in front of where I sat, and planted her hands on the arms of the chair, boxing me in. "We don't have much time. You have to listen to me right now."

"Where *were you?*" I couldn't keep the accusation from my tone. Amy had *suffered* while they were *planning*, and my rage at my mate's pain couldn't be contained. She never believed this would be over, and I watched her over Erica's shoulder as Misha helped her from the chair. Amy's entire body trembled as shock, disbelief, and relief flooded her at once.

"We're sorry," Erica scrambled through an explanation. "We had to gather supplies. Now, *please listen,* Eldich." I shifted my gaze to Erica only when she stamped her foot in frustration. "The rubaee poison won't kill us, but it'll drug us. We have minutes, tops, before Tori and I become a drunken mess. You must get us outside, *all of us.* Do you understand?"

"What's the plan?"

"Get. Us. *Outside,*" Erica hissed the instructions through gritted teeth as she leaned forward, and her fingers gripped the arms of the chair.

"Tell me the plan!" But Erica's eyes glazed over, and she froze in that position, looking at but not seeing me. "Erica?" I whispered. When I glanced at Tori, she was also standing still, staring at the wall as a vacant smile spread across her lips.

"This place is so shiny," she whispered.

Erica whirled around to face Tori. "I knooow." She approached Tori, stumbled in her steps, and laughed before she grabbed Tori's shoulder. "Hey… hey, do you know what would be really fun right about now?"

"What?"

"A water balloon fight."

Tori let out an exaggerated gasp. "Oh my God, you're a *genius.*"

Erica's brows pulled together as she frowned. "Wasn't there something we were supposed to do?"

"Giant alien cock!" Tori yelled, and Erica spit as she burst into laughter.

"But we already did that."

I had too many questions, no time, and no one to ask, so I had no choice but to follow Erica's instructions and hope there was more to this plan than to simply run.

"Come on, girls. Time to go outside," I said as I strode toward them and held my arms out, indicating the door.

"Who's the new guy?" Erica asked as she nudged Tori with her elbow.

Tori smirked. "I dunno. He's cute. Not as cute as my vine man, though. *Hey.* Did I tell you what he can do with his vines—"

"We're going to go outside and play with water balloons," I snapped. I had no idea what *water balloons* were, but if it got the girls outside, then mission accomplished.

Erica clapped her hands together and jumped up and down on the spot. "Really?"

"Yes, really, but you've got to go right now."

Instead of running, Tori and Erica turned toward each other, clapping their hands and doing a strange dance. I ran my hand down my face before turning to the other women.

"Misha, Tegan, grab Erica and Tori and get them outside." Misha sprung into action, grabbed Tegan's arm before she could question, and pulled her toward her friends. They had to coax them outside with gentle talk and promises of whatever nonsense they were asking for.

Tegan and Misha grabbed their shoulders and steered them toward the exit from the lab while Erica and Tori cooed at every piece of equipment they passed. "Ooh shiny…"

"Amy," I turned and held out my hand. "Let's go."

Her eyes shone with emotion, and even though she trembled as she reached out for me, she nodded with determination as she took my hand.

CHAPTER 16

ELDICH

The second we were through the doors from the lab and into the open, Erica and Tori again bolted in opposite directions.

"Where are you going?" I shouted, but they were giggling and racing around in circles in the space between the buildings, throwing their arms over their heads and flapping their hands about.

"Shit," Misha said. She stood with her knees slightly bent, her eyes moving in a constant circle around the center of the colony where we stood, searching. The Ghaal were dotted around, watching us wearily. "They won't watch forever.

We've got to move."

I ushered Amy gently toward Tegan and Misha. "Run into the forest. I'll get Tori and Erica."

"Did they tell you the plan?" Amy asked, biting her bottom lip.

"No," I snarled out. Erica had only told me to get everyone outside. *I'd done that—now what?* My instinct was to run, but I had to save my brothers' mates. "Just head toward the forest and keep running. I'll find you."

"But—"

Amy's dispute over my instruction was cut off by a strangled cry from a Ghaal. We turned to see him pulling a barb of some sort from his thigh. My eyes narrowed, seeking Erica and Tori out. They were heading toward the forest, and I sighed in relief. If they could get lost within the trees, we could find them later, as long as they were safe from the Ghaal.

The Ghaal inspected the barb he pulled from his leg, his eyes going wide with rage when recognition hit seconds before he collapsed to the ground. Elation filled my chest, and while I never wanted to feel joy at the pain of others, this was incredible.

My brothers and the humans had weaponized eylak venom—small creatures that lived in the sandy soils around the other side of the mountains between Lanir's territory and mine. They'd shoot up a venomous barb when something stepped on the sand, and once knocked out, they'd consume their victim.

The venom was enough to kill a Ghaal and take a Synth out for days.

But the Ghaal was in for a slow death. Unlike the rubaee that went straight for the heart, the eylak venom would first paralyze until breathing became impossible.

The eylaks liked their meat warm.

A whirring shot past my shoulder, and I turned as another Ghaal was hit by a barb.

I couldn't contain my grin. "My brothers," I murmured. Spinning, I grabbed Amy's shoulders and pointed her toward the trees where the barb had been shot from. "Head toward those trees."

"Something is shooting at us!"

"Not us, *them.* My brothers are there. Now *go.*"

Amy hesitated and stood staring at me until Misha started running and grabbed Tegan and Amy's hands as she moved past. The Ghaal realized the females were escaping and bolted after them. Several were taken down by barbs, and they split up to circle around the women.

I snarled, about to pursue when I witnessed several more taken down by the barbs, and turned to make sure Tori and Erica had made it to safety.

Terror, confusion, and anger rose in my chest as I fisted my hands at my sides. Erica and Tori were still racing around in circles about the colony, but now their arms were full of gladvin berries.

Frowning, I watched them for a moment. The berries weren't almost clear with a yellow tinge as they should be but looked like they'd been filled with something gray.

Erica screamed with delight as a group of Ghaal stopped just short of her, and before they could advance, she tossed one of the berries at them. It exploded on contact, soaking two Ghaal in the gray liquid. Seconds later, they fell to their knees before one crumpled forward first, his face hitting the ground with a thud as the other fell back, clutching his chest.

They'd filled the berries with rubaee poison.

"Water balloon fight!" Erica declared, throwing another at the group that circled her, taking out three.

There was chaos as Erica and Tori ran around throwing poison at the Ghaal. Several more were taken out by the barbs, and I stood in indecision. There was a plan, and I had no idea what it was and what role I played in it. Screaming behind me had me whirling around again. Misha had been grabbed from behind, and her feet lifted from the ground as she fought against the Ghaal.

Where is Amy?

As I was about to head toward Misha, Erica ran past me, pulled her tunic over her head, and exposed her breasts as she ran. Several of the Ghaal paused in their pursuit, their eyes dropping to her body as she ran past. One took after her, his fingers grazing her hair as he got close to grabbing her.

"You can't touch me! I'm *poisonous. Ha ha haa!*"

"Erica…" I snarled her name out, running a palm down my face before taking chase. There is no way her getting naked in front of the Ghaal was part of the plan.

Where are my brothers?

I tackled the Ghaal behind Erica, grabbed and snapped his neck before I pushed myself to my feet, and took off after Erica again. A second wave of Ghaal burst from the lab, and I launched myself at Erica, covering her with my body as we rolled to a stop. She squirmed in my arms, her eyes wide. "Don't touch me, I'm poison!" I growled as I let her go. She rolled off me and stilled for a few shuddering seconds, waiting for signs I'd been poisoned by the rubaee plant.

Nothing.

Releasing a breath, I stood. "Erica," I hissed her name out and clapped my large hands in front of her face. "Look at me. What's the plan?"

Her eyes were out of focus. "We're gonna get taken…" she whispered in a sing-song voice.

"What?"

A small smile played on her lips. "Just let it happen. Trust me, sexy alien man."

"*Stop!*"

I turned slowly at the Ghaal's command, blocking

Erica from them with my body as I held my hands out. From the corner of my vision, I could see Tori still throwing the poisoned berries at any Ghaal who came near her, and Erica giggled behind my back. Several Ghaal were brandishing the weapons they needed to kill Synths, and I stilled. My stomach churned as my chest tightened. I *hated* they had this one bit of control over us. The only reason I didn't rush them now was because of Amy. Had she made it to safety? Last I saw, she was running toward the trees as directed. But Misha had been grabbed again. Did they get Amy too?

Either way, she'd need me, and I couldn't risk my life to take out a handful of Ghaal while she waited for me.

Glancing around the center of the colony, I couldn't help but smirk. The ground was littered with the bodies of Ghaal, both male and what few females they had left. They now had Tori and were wearing protective gloves as they worked to keep her still. There were several of the poison-filled berries abandoned on the ground near her, and she was laughing hysterically as they pinned her on her stomach with her arms behind her back, her feet kicking wildly.

How many Ghaal had the females managed to kill—two dozen, perhaps more?

There couldn't be more than a handful of them left.

My gaze returned to the nameless Ghaal in front of me—they may as well be faceless too. I didn't care to learn one from the other. None of them deserved to live.

"I won't come back with you," I growled out the words and stepped back, which also forced Erica to step backward.

"We don't care. Just give us the female. You're useless." He spat at my feet. "We gave you more than enough chances to fuck the female, and you didn't. *Leave*. We're closer now than we've ever been."

My brows pulled together. *Closer?*

Erica stepped out from behind me. "I want to be with my friends," she declared.

A Ghaal sneered. "So, come with us."

My hand shot out to grab Erica, and she dodged me. As she walked past, her head was tilted almost comically to the side, and she whispered, "Trust me…" as she went to the Ghaal. Two of them went to grab her, and she lifted her arms in the air. "Ah-ah-ah, I'm poisonous, remember?"

There was a smattering of angry chatter, and they settled for holding her at the point of their weapons.

There was no more reason for them to keep me alive.

As one lunged for me, I jumped backward and ran without looking back, hating myself more for every step I took away from the colony.

I need to live for Amy.

It was the only thought that kept me going.

Deeper into the woodlands, I slowed. I wasn't being pursued. With so few Ghaal left, I doubted they would spare any of them to worry about me anyway. My chest ached, and I looked around the sparsely lit area. The sunlight had broken amongst the treetops, and I wanted to call for Amy.

But if she was near, I didn't want to give her location away either.

Inhaling deeply, I caught the hint of a feminine scent and moved toward it. Following the trail had me skirting around the forest parallel to the colony but not farther away from it. As I got closer, I recognized the scent as it intensified with a spike of fear and sweat.

Not Amy.

Snarling, I reached into a well left by the large roots of the trees and grabbed Tegan's arm. As she opened her mouth to scream, I slapped my hand over her face. "It's me." When her struggles didn't stop, I forced calm into my voice. The female was panicked and didn't need me snarling against her ear. "It's Eldich. You're safe." Eventually, Tegan relaxed into my arms, but she continued to tremble as her chest rose and fell with her harsh breathing. I released Tegan and turned her to face me, her eyes and cheeks red from crying. "Where is Amy?"

"I don't know," she whispered, sniffing. "You told us to run, and I ran." She studied me for a moment. "Why are you so obsessed with her?"

"She's my mate."

Tegan opened her mouth to answer but instead squealed at the sound of approaching footsteps and ducked behind me. I crouched, cursing how my skin color made me stand out in this forest. This wasn't the environment I had adapted to, and the sandy yellow of my skin made my position obvious amongst the deep greens that surrounded me.

"Eldich," Samara exclaimed as she rushed toward me. "You're safe." I stood and stepped to the side to reveal Tegan behind me. Tegan's eyes widened at the sight of another human, and she immediately stepped forward to stand next to her instead of me. "I'm Samara," she said, offering Tegan her hand.

"Tegan." They clasped hands for a moment and stilled before Samara yanked her forward into a hug.

Tegan's shoulders shuddered as the tears came, and Samara shushed her gently. "Are you okay?"

"I am now..." Tegan's voice broke as she

answered. "Aren't I?"

"Yes, you're safe now." Samara looked at me as I took her in. She had a tube that looked like a hollowed-out reed hanging from her wrist by a small tie and a small bag that still contained a handful of eylak barbs. She had been the one firing. "Come," she said, and I followed, but my steps were stilted and stiff as I struggled to contain my rage.

I had questions, but Samara was not the one to ask, so I followed her without saying anything. If the females had indeed attacked without the knowledge of my brothers, then my brothers were fools for allowing them to get so far. On the other hand, if all of this was part of a plan, the fact the females had been sent in without my brothers to protect them filled me with rage. My hands curled into fists at my sides, and I kept my distance behind Samara and Tegan, not wanting to unleash my anger unjustly onto them.

Before long, we reached a small clearing, and I stopped short at the sight of all five of my brothers. Before anyone could speak, the growl in my chest started and increased, and I roared my frustration at them. A single note of anger and pain. I slammed a palm to my chest as my gaze darted around, but I couldn't see Amy.

Tegan's eyes were wide as she stepped behind Samara, and they edged closer to Lanir.

"*That* was the plan?" I yelled, throwing my arms

up before getting closer to Ilk, and I jabbed a finger against his chest. "*Where is Amy?*"

Samara answered, clearing her throat uncertainly. "Captured again, I think. Only Tegan and I are here."

I roared and gripped my hair with my fingers. The rage the Ghaal had been building in me for days came to the surface, and with nowhere else to direct it, I launched myself at Ilk. My hands hit his shoulders, and he fell beneath my weight. Tegan's scream barely registered with me before there were arms around my shoulders, neck, and chest, pulling me back and holding me still.

"What's the plan, Ilk? *What is the plan?*" I fought against Ryth and Lanir's hold. "Who knows what they'll do to them now? Why would they keep waiting for six?"

"They'll be safe until they have six."

I wanted to rip my hair out. The growl was rumbling through my chest so loud now it was drowning out all other thoughts beyond saving Amy.

Amy.

My mate.

The Ghaal held their superstition in high accord, but now their numbers had been easily *halved* in one day, if not more. They wouldn't wait any longer, especially now they had four of the six females. Surely, they would say it would be good enough to begin their experimentation.

"Eldich, *please...*" Samara's voice trembled with unshed tears, even as she straightened her back to face me. Lanir eyed me with a snarl of his own, which I returned with equal vigor. It was no fault of mine his mate was upset. *He* was the one who had let her friends go in alone. "We had to thin their numbers. If the Synths had gone in, the Ghaal would have been immediately in defense mode. With Erica and Tori, while they would've still been suspicious, they could get much further into the colony without a counterattack. The Ghaal have a weapon against the Synths, but they wouldn't kill us. Did you see how many we Ghaal we took down?" Samara approached me, and Lanir growled as she placed a hand on my chest. Her expression was clear, and I ceased my struggles against my brothers, who continued to hold me. "Did you *see?* Dozens are dead..."

"I can't believe you let them do this," I muttered, snarling at Ilk when he lifted a lip in a growl at me.

"We didn't *want* them to. It was their plan, and it made the most sense."

Samara ignored the exchange and continued, "And now that's done, we're going straight back in."

"*What?*" Tegan took a step back, her voice shrill and hands shaking. "I'm not going back in there."

"We have to," Samara pleaded with her. "One last time, I promise. It'll be over soon."

"*No,*" Tegan cried out, moving away from her. Her gaze darted around my brothers, and she seemed unsure who to take shelter behind, apparently not trusting any of us. Eventually, her eyes settled on me, and she hesitantly shuffled closer to me as she spoke to Samara, "I don't want a part in any more of this. I just want to go home. I don't want to be captured, and I don't want to be pregnant with some alien baby like that Misha girl!"

There was a beat of silence as we stilled.

A rumbling growl started in Sahcor's chest, louder than mine, as though a storm was brewing inside him. "Misha is pregnant?"

"Did the Ghaal..." Vitri's eyes were wide, unable to finish the question.

Tegan lifted a hand over her mouth as all six of us stared at her. Sahcor advanced a step which she instinctively retreated from. "N-no," she whispered at Vitri before she pointed at Sahcor. "She said it's his."

"Sahcor..." Ilk's voice was edged in warning as he watched his brother's chest rise and fall with heavy breaths, each one ending in a grunt as Sahcor began growling.

"*My child.* My mate is pregnant with my child!" Sahcor snarled at Ilk's warning before his gaze settled back on Tegan. "We go now." Sahcor grunted, his teeth grinding together as his jaw tightened. "*Now.*"

Samara was trembling even as she nodded, and she reached out to intertwine her fingers with Lanir's. The gesture was so pure my chest ached. "Yes," she whispered. She barely managed to pull a smile together as she smoothed Lanir's brow with her thumb. "You gotta tie me up. It's gotta look real."

"Someone better tell me the plan *right now.*" I snarled, baring my teeth at my brothers. Tegan had backed away from all of us by now, and when Ryth approached her, she tried to shove him away, squealing when he grabbed her arm. My eyes met his before I noted the tremble in his fingers as he crouched next to Tegan and whispered things to her. She stopped pulling against his hold, but the tears streaming down her cheeks continued as she glared at him.

"You'd *know* the plan if you didn't *sneak* off." Vitri shoved me in the shoulder, his growls matching mine.

"I'm going to get Misha."

"Sahcor, we have to stick to the plan." Samara stood in front of him, holding her small hands out as if she had a chance of keeping him back with force. The height difference between them was enunciated as he towered over her, but she tilted her head up to look at him. "If Misha is pregnant, she'll be safe, right? They won't need to make her *more* pregnant."

"And they won't touch Erica or Tori for a few

hours," Vitri added, taking a deep breath as if he were trying to convince himself as well as us. He glared at me again before sighing as though he was trying to center himself. "They'll want to make sure the effects of the poison have worn off first."

"So, what you're saying…" I pulled the words out as a cavern opened in my chest. I shoved Vitri away from me with my elbow, even though he was no longer holding me back. "That the only one in immediate danger if the Ghaal decide to forgo their superstitions is Amy?"

There was another beat of silence where the drum of my heart sounded in my ears, and Samara's gentle voice barely managed to break through the haze fogging my mind. "We're heading back in now. Our plan will work."

"What makes you so sure?" I snarled, hating that she recoiled from me and had to ignore Lanir's challenging scowl.

"Because they have help."

Tegan screamed as a Ghaal stepped into the clearing.

CHAPTER 17

AMY

The excited chattering of the Ghaal churned my stomach more than the sounds their bodies had made when they'd hit the ground. There had been carnage in the village when Erica and Tori ran around and threw poison at the Ghaal as well as someone firing some sort of darts at them from beyond the tree line. I'd run with Tegan and Misha as Eldich had directed. Even though it had been against my instinct to run *toward* the origin of the darts, he was right—they weren't firing at us.

Tegan's hand had slipped from mine when she surged ahead, and I'd cried out as I was tackled from the side. I was so close to the trees my fingers were almost brushing them, and Tegan stopped and turned as I was crushed to the ground by two Ghaal. We shared a moment of pained eye contact, where she glanced between me and the trees beyond.

"Run!" I kicked out, my foot collided with the jaw of a Ghaal, and I screamed at the pain of his sharp cheekbone against my bare foot. Amongst the chaos, I searched for Eldich, but he'd disappeared. Tegan's hesitation took seconds too long, and she screamed as a Ghaal gripped her upper arm and hissed at her.

"Tegan, *run,*" I cried out again, desperate to break her from the shock that held her in place. Tegan's eyes widened before she tugged herself free from the Ghaal's grip, spun on her heel, and bolted, twisting and turning between the thick trunks of the trees and into the darkness they provided. When the Ghaal went to go after her, I lunged, grabbed his ankle, and shrieked as he fell and rolled, twisting my arm awkwardly. I was grabbed by more Ghaal, and the one I'd tripped yelled words I couldn't understand in my face before he landed a slap on my cheek so hard I tasted blood. Misha had also disappeared beyond the wall of Ghaals that surrounded us, and I could only hope Tegan had found her way to safety.

Was this their plan?

Where is Eldich?

Where are his brothers?

Eldich seemed so sure they would come to save us, but in the end, it was the other abducted women who came instead. As I was dragged to my feet, I struggled to wrap my head around what had gone down. So much had happened so fast. Erica and Tori had somehow poisoned the Ghaal with something that was deadly to them but only made the girls act like they were drunk. We had to practically herd them out of the lab, and the second they were in the daylight, they bolted again, uncontrollable and unpredictable.

Then they reappeared from the trees with poison-filled water balloons, or that's what they seemed like at least, and had taken down more Ghaal.

But there was no sign of more Synths. I didn't know exactly what they looked like other than Sahcor, but I'd seen no giant male aliens other than the Ghaal. Eldich had disappeared, and I bit my lip against any rising emotion, hoping they hadn't captured him again.

After the attack, any torture they inflicted on him would surely kill him.

I slumped against the Ghaal's hold as I was dragged back toward the lab, where they tied me up in the corner and made me wait while chaos continued to reign outside.

Eventually, I was taken into the cell I'd been held

in previously. Misha was there, and her cheeks were flushed and red from anger or exertion—I couldn't tell. She held my gaze over where Tori and Erica bent in front of her to fuss over her stomach as they poked at her belly gently and made cooing sounds. Misha's expression was blank, and I slowly closed my eyes, turned my head upward, and took a deep breath as the cell door was locked behind me.

Whatever the plan was, it doesn't seem like it went well.

The day started with three of us in captivity…

… now, there were four.

The excited chatter of the Ghaal continued, and they changed their language so we could understand.

"We have more of them now than we did before the escape attempt."

"Don't get complacent. This might be part of their plan."

"We'll be on high alert. The Synths won't get anywhere near us."

"What if the other two females return?"

"Let them. We'll be ready."

They chuckled amongst themselves, and my shoulders slumped.

"Fuck you," Misha spat the words at them, but they ignored her as they slowly filtered out of the hallway and back into the lab before they closed the door behind them, leaving us alone again.

"Shh…" Tori pressed her finger against Misha's lips as she straightened, effectively smooshing Misha's face up. "Fuck's a naughty word."

Erica gasped. "You said it too!"

"I did? Fuck!"

"What's wrong with them?" I asked Misha.

She lifted a shoulder. "Drugged somehow. Apparently, whatever they used to kill the Ghaal doesn't kill us."

I nodded, even though she wasn't telling me anything I didn't already guess myself. I had hoped Misha would have some additional information, but the only ones who would be able to answer my questions were currently unable to answer anything coherently.

"I can't believe you've got a baby in there," Tori cooed at Misha's stomach.

"An *alien* baby," Erica added.

"A water nymph baby." Tori cackled.

Erica joined in with a giggle. "I am *so* horny right now."

"*Girl,* me too."

"Shush, both of you," Misha snapped as she shoved them away from her and approached me. "I don't buy for a second this was the entire plan. They're definitely coming back."

"Whatever the plan was, I don't think it worked." I sighed and leaned against the cell's cold wall.

Misha tapped my temple as a hint of a smile tugged at her lips. "Don't think like that. Did you look around outside? Bodies left and right. These two idiots must've halved the colony's numbers in less than a day."

"I guess…"

"This was only step one. Trust me on this. We'll have to wait for Erica and Tori to sober up before we can find out more, but somehow, I doubt we'll be waiting long."

"Your knight in shining armor will come for you?" My lip twisted in a sarcastic smile, but Misha's face lit up with the promise of possibility.

"And yours."

"Against the wall." We jumped back as a Ghaal entered through the door at the end of the hall and snapped at us. He held a barrel with a hose end in it and pointed it at us. "We can't do much until the poison is out of their system." He nodded at Tori and Erica, who were giggling and playing some clapping game with their hands. "But we can wash you down and make sure there are no more surprises."

"Wha—" The pressure from the water knocked me off my feet, and I screamed, holding my hands out in front of my face as the water blasted toward me. The Ghaal waved the barrel back and forth, soaking the four of us as we cowered against the rear wall. The water had an orange tinge to it and smelled like antiseptic. I was thankful it didn't burn, but the pressure alone was enough to leave my skin stinging.

He washed us thoroughly and left us drenched, leaning against the wall as he exited the hallway.

"That guy is terrible at surprise parties," Erica muttered.

I almost laughed.

ELDICH

"Let him go, Eldich," Ilk's commanding voice rang out, but I didn't let up, my forearm pressed against the throat of the Ghaal who had dared come near us, his back against a thick tree.

"Eldich!" Samara cried out, and the pressure I was exuding against the Ghaal's throat loosened slightly at her voice. This drew another snarl from my throat—I never wanted to do anything to upset or harm the females, *especially* my Amy. I was reacting to Samara with the same instinct and found myself backing off the moment there was a hint of distress in her voice. "He's helping us. Let him go." This time, her words were delivered calmly, but with the same authority Ilk spoke with.

I narrowed my eyes at the Ghaal, and he held my gaze. After another moment, I released my hold on him and let him drop to the ground as he gripped his throat, coughing hoarsely. Samara hovered near him, looking like she was about to reach out a hand to help him up, but at the last moment, she pulled away and retreated to be next to Lanir.

She was still afraid of him. Regardless of whatever help he offered, the Ghaal frightened her.

Tegan was hiding behind Ryth, and he had one arm behind him, keeping her tucked against his back as she peeked out in the gap between his torso and elbow.

I turned to Ilk. "Explain."

"Sol came to us," he started, not helping the Ghaal up, but instead, Ilk simply watched as he stood and continued to rub his neck. I held no guilt for the pain I'd inflicted on him, and the air of distrust that flowed around us all only put me further on edge. This Ghaal, Sol, was apparently helping us, but we could never fully trust him. "He'd been in captivity himself since he helped Erica escape."

My eyes darted to Sol, and he held my gaze and offered a single solemn nod. "I was put into a cell with Misha, told to mate her or be killed." Sahcor snarled, and Sol flinched. "I didn't touch her. I didn't want to hurt anyone anymore." His eyes found mine as if pleading for me to forgive him, even though he knew I never could. Not for what had been done to us, and especially never on behalf of the females. "They set Misha up with an apparent means to escape. She took it and begged me to do the same before she ran. I wasn't going to, but then I realized whatever fate awaited me out here was the same as what awaited me in the colony… death." He turned away from me and gazed at each of us in turn. "I wandered for days before I came across Ilk's home, but even then, I didn't go to him straight away. I was certain you would kill me the second you saw me."

"I would have," Lanir snarled out, and Sol nodded as though expecting nothing less.

"When I finally approached and saw you gathering together, I knew you were planning something. My life was spared only because Erica recognized me. So, I offered my assistance in ending this." His jaw tightened before he added, "I won't survive this, but if my final act is to be a part in ending the horrors I helped create, then it will be a worthy death."

There was no sympathy in me, and death was the very best he deserved. I punched the tree next to his head, and while Sol's jaw ticked, he didn't flinch. "What will the Ghaal do now?" I demanded.

"Double down. They'll protect the numbers they have left. There will be upset within the ranks now, and there will be those who'll push for impregnation to begin immediately, regardless of the missing two."

Before I could speak again, Ilk's hand landed on my shoulder. "I never planned to leave my mate in the hands of the Ghaal for a second longer than necessary. We will go now."

I said nothing and turned to find Samara and Tegan being loosely bound in rope. Tegan was openly crying, which I'm sure would play into the idea she had been captured against her will. Even Samara's façade of strength was wavering, and she kept her gaze resolutely on Lanir as he tied her arms to her sides, the rumble of his growl low and constant.

CHAPTER
18

AMY

"Get up."

My head jerked up as a Ghaal barked the order at us from outside the cell. There were at least a dozen of them standing on the other side of the bars, and my brows drew together as I took in each of them in turn. They all carried bags slung over their shoulders and had weapons at the ready. Several had long poles with ropes tied into nooses at the end, while others held those horrible cattle-prod things they'd used on Eldich.

"Up!" he screamed, and I scrambled to my feet. Erica and Tori were slower to respond, and while they seemed to have gone past the silly and unpredictable stage of the poison, they were now barely conscious, and Misha and I had to drag them to their feet. Tori's legs gave out from underneath her, and with her arm slung over my shoulder, my legs buckled at the sudden drop of her weight.

The cell door slid open following the clicks of the locks releasing, and the Ghaal surrounded us, weapons pointed at the ready. "Get her on her feet," one snapped at me.

"I'm trying," I pleaded. But Tori was going limp in my arms, slipping from my grip as I struggled to keep her upright. Misha had a firm grip on Erica's waist, but Erica's head lolled, and Misha almost stumbled as they swayed to the side.

"They're practically unconscious," Misha spat at the Ghaal. "We can't carry them."

There was a burst of angry chattering from the Ghaal, and a couple of them darted off into the lab, returning shortly with stretchers of some sort.

"Secure them."

The Ghaal stood back and watched us as Misha and I dragged Erica and Tori onto the stretchers and secured them with the straps. The Ghaal weren't helping, evidently still unsure about getting too close to them. Surely, they weren't *actually* poisonous. Otherwise, the Ghaal would've been dropping dead when they held them still in the lab in the first place.

Although I barely contained my smirk. I guess they would be extra careful now because of the number of Ghaal they'd lost.

I hated the idea I was reveling in the death and suffering of others, but from not only what I'd been told, but experienced firsthand, the Ghaal was a cruel species. They viewed all others as below them and seemed to think they could use them as they pleased, including us.

I worked my bottom lip between my teeth as I secured Tori, trying to make sure she would be safe and comfortable on the stretcher. It occurred to me the Synths' plan would be to kill *all* of the Ghaal, and I wasn't sure how I felt about that. I didn't want to be anywhere near them, but to wipe an entire species from the face of the planet? That was a big call to make.

"Turn around."

When I took too long to respond, a Ghaal jabbed the prod into my stomach, and I buckled with the pain. Misha gave my arm an encouraging squeeze and nodded firmly before we both stood and turned our backs to the Ghaal. The stretchers were lifted and secured to our shoulders, and I slumped under the weight.

"Walk."

Where are we going?

I knew there was no point in asking the Ghaal.

Was this *part of the girls' plan?*

Certain Misha was thinking the same thing, we shared an uneasy glance as we were marched out of the cell and down the opposite end of the hallway. The hall twisted a few corners, and the straps from the stretcher were already digging into my shoulders. I screamed as an explosion rocked the building and ducked when dust and debris fell from the ceiling around us.

"Keep moving."

Misha adjusted Erica's stretcher on her shoulders and surged ahead. She kept glancing at me as if she wanted to say something but thought the better of it. I doubted Misha knew any more than I did, so I simply shook my head slightly and kept pace with her as we trudged through the hallway.

When we reached a large door, the Ghaal in front of us opened it, and the sunlight assaulted my eyes. They pointed outside, and we moved, feeling the ground change beneath our feet from the smooth, cool material of the Ghaal building to the compacted soil of the village ground. We headed for the trees, and my heart pounded in my chest.

Should I make a run for it?

My question was answered as the stretcher holding Tori slid over a bump in the ground, and the twist of the weight almost brought me to my knees again. No. There's no way I could run and take Tori with me, and Misha had Erica.

I wasn't going to leave them all behind.

Somewhere out there was Tegan, Eldich, and his brothers, and I knew he wouldn't leave me.

When we passed between two trees, I had to stop and take in my surroundings. I could have sworn we were moving farther into the forest, but the second we passed between these two trees, I was in another hallway, this one sloping steadily downward underground.

"Move," a Ghaal hissed and poked me with the prod, but no shock was given. I took the hint and kept moving, glancing behind me to see almost two dozen Ghaal following us. They were loaded up, carrying bags and equipment, and over their heads, I could see smoke coming from the buildings behind us.

The tunnel darkened as it continued to slope downward, and another explosion had me ducking again. The ground shuddered, and I pulled Misha down by her wrist. We crouched like that, foreheads close together as I clamped my hands over my ears. Another explosion echoed around me, and we coughed through the dust.

When I glanced up, the Ghaal around us lit torches, and through the beams, I could see the cave-in behind us.

I didn't know where they were taking us, but it seemed they were covering their tracks.

We walked.

The skin on my shoulders was rubbed raw from dragging the stretcher, and no amount of rolling my shoulders and adjusting the weight eased the pain.

"Misha," I whispered, and she glanced up at me. "Where are they taking us?"

"I don't know," she admitted, and while I wasn't expecting any other answer, it didn't stop my stomach from sinking as the last bit of hope I had gave way.

"Do you think this was what the girls' planned?"

Misha shook her head even as she said, "I hope so."

"They're no longer waiting, you know." I jumped at the sound of the voice to my left and shifted closer to Misha as a Ghaal stared intently at me. Taking her in, I noticed her thicker eyelashes and the swell of two small breasts on her chest under her simple tunic.

"Wh-what?" I stuttered out. I couldn't trust this Ghaal just because she was female, and the wicked grin she gave me when I had responded to her only cemented my suspicions.

"They're not going to wait until they have all six of you anymore. Rah and many of the others who held these beliefs so highly have been killed, and any left who care have been subdued. Those who remain are of the belief our species is worth the risk of impregnation without six." When I tried to move away from her, she reached out and gripped my upper arm, digging her sharp nails into my skin. The orange rings of her irises flashed dangerously as she smiled again. "Still, they'll take minor precautions, offering up two female Ghaal to be impregnated with you humans, even though they know it won't work." She laughed, and my skin crawled where she touched me. "It's a technicality, but I think they're beyond caring now."

I ripped my arm from her grip, only to have her hand latch around my throat.

"Let her go," Misha screamed and attempted to dig her fingers into the female's eyes. The Ghaal shoved her, Misha stumbled with the weight of the stretcher, and Erica's unconscious form rolled dangerously to the side.

"The little stunt your friends pulled achieved only one thing... ensuring your future. Did you think we'd wait around for them to come back? Those who were stupid enough to bring them into the lab in the first place without restraining them are dead, and I'm glad of it."

I couldn't speak and clawed at her hand around my throat.

"The moment we arrive in our other lab, you and

these two…" she waved a hand at Tori and Erica, "… will be impregnated. The Ghaal will live on."

"I don't like this," another Ghaal muttered behind us. "The sacred number has never let us down before."

"Oh, shut it, Ith!"

"Think about it." He gestured vaguely around. "There are thirty-six of us remaining, including the humans. That's exactly six lots of six. Do you think that's a coincidence? It's a sign."

There was a smattering of mutters and some scoffs in response to this, and I stilled. Their beliefs were the only hope I had of being safe for a while longer at the other end of this tunnel. But my stomach still churned. Because this wasn't just about me—Erica and Tori were in as much danger as I was. As soon as they woke up and the poison was out of their system, they'd be fair game too.

Another male Ghaal stepped forward and slid a blade out from his pocket. He slashed at the arm of the Ghaal who'd spoken, and a splatter of gray blood sprayed across my legs as I flinched. "Shut it, Ith," the Ghaal snarled out. "Or they'll be thirty-five of us. Keep moving."

The female Ghaal shoved me to the side, and I stumbled, twisting my knee painfully as Tori's unconscious weight tilted me. Sounds surrounded me—Ghaal shouting at me to get back up, laughter, and Misha fighting off one who'd dared to touch her—but I couldn't make sense of anything beyond the buzzing that filled my head. My eyes filled with tears, and I blinked them away angrily. Eldich had promised we'd be rescued, but now we were being taken away from the colony to God knows where, and we were no longer hanging by the thread of safety that was the Ghaal's superstitions.

Misha was trying to catch my eye as we stood again and readjusted the stretchers, but I kept my gaze firmly on the floor in front of me.

I was a fool to have thought this was over.

ELDICH

As Ilk and Lanir flanked Sol, I lingered back with Vitri and Ryth.

Sahcor was well ahead, and I'd lost sight of him between the thick trees several minutes ago. Tegan was still whimpering, and every now and then would twist her arms and loosen the knots that had been tied to give the illusion she had been captured. Each time she did this, we'd have to stop and redo the knots, and she'd sob again. I ground my teeth together—the idea of using the females as bait didn't sit right with me. I acknowledged the first part of their plan was well done, and the number of

Ghaal Erica, Tori, and Samara had managed to take out was impressive. The remaining numbers wouldn't have much of a chance against us, and I was happy to simply storm the colony with Lanir and Sahcor and kill the remaining with my bare hands.

But Samara didn't want that.

She was afraid her friends would get hurt or killed in the confusion and wanted to be taken to them first so she could make sure they were safe and huddled together before we attacked.

I understood and was thankful. But then I'd remember how the Ghaal had strapped Amy down to the chair in front of me and spread her legs. I recalled the threats they'd made against her and the danger they'd put her in, and my fingers would twitch against my palms.

The problem with creating a being that could be trained to run on pure instinct was that instinct couldn't always be directed where they wanted it. The desire to mate was strong, but stronger than that was the desire to *protect* my mate. And if that meant tearing every Ghaal who stood in my way from limb to limb, then I would feel no guilt for that, even as their blood soaked me and the sound of their bones crunching filled my senses.

We had been passive for too long, and I was also to blame. I was far enough from the colony I could almost get lost in my solidarity and imagine I had a life outside the duty my brothers and I had taken on. I'd been on the outside—not tortured as much as Lanir and not witnessing as much as Ilk—and seeing Amy had been like a switch flicked inside me.

"Send them back to your cave," I muttered, and Ilk turned to face me.

"What?"

"Tegan and Samara, send them back to your cave. We can end this without them."

Lanir snarled and nodded, scowling at Samara. Evidently, he would do anything for her, even go against his protective instinct to help her and do things her way because it made her happy.

I tilted my chin at Sol. "Send him in alone. He can check on the women."

Sol shook his head. "If I go in there alone, they'll kill me on sight. I can get the females into the lab. Once I'm in, I can release the others and get them all to safety." He eyed me. "But I have no chance of getting close to them, including Amy, if I don't have Samara and Tegan with me. They're the key to me getting in."

I snarled at his use of Amy's name, which was intended to nudge me into compliance. "The other Ghaal have no reason to trust you."

"You're right. This is why we'll move quickly." He glanced at Ilk. "Your plan was good, using the females to enter the colony and thin their numbers, but they'll be on edge now. They'll kill a Synth immediately. I, however, just may be able to make it in far enough to free the females, even if I die doing it."

"We've been over this," Vitri said, pushing his hand between my shoulder blades as we started walking again. "I don't like it either. Remember, it's not only your mate in there."

I paused and tilted my head toward the sky as Lanir did the same. His hand landed on Samara's shoulder and squeezed.

"Smoke," he grunted. Without another word, he lifted Samara over his shoulder and bolted toward the colony, and I followed without looking back.

We stopped at the edge of the woodlands and simply stared at the sight in front of us.

The entire colony was up in flames.

Every building that wasn't already collapsed was crumbling into itself, and the heat from the flames could be felt from where we stood. Thick black smoke clouded the sky above us, and Tegan flinched behind me when the crash of another roof collapsing shook the ground.

"Was this part of the plan?" I asked as Ryth

pushed his way past me and watched the destruction.

Lanir rounded on Sol, grabbed the front of his clothing, and yanked him to his feet. "Where have they gone?" We all knew the women would be with the Ghaal. They were too precious for them to leave behind, and this was designed to leave us no clues.

"I-I don't know. Rah never mentioned…" Sol's eyes were wide, and he grunted as Lanir dropped him to the ground.

Samara wiggled out of the loose ropes around her, and Tegan immediately followed suit before she kicked them away from her and huffed out an angry breath.

"Where would they have taken them?" Samara asked, her eyes wide as their plan collapsed around them.

"We pushed their hand," Sahcor said, staring ahead of him as some of the flames burned down into embers around the nearest building. "I knew they'd want to begin impregnation quickly after their numbers were so drastically cut. But—"

"But you didn't think they'd have an alternative place to take them," Ryth added.

Sahcor's jaw tensed. "Their technology was dying. I watched them try to fix things as they broke down for years. All the technology specialists are long dead, and all their working technology is *here*. It doesn't make any sense. If they had another lab, why would they keep trying to fix this one?"

"Lanir..." Samara wrapped her small hand around Lanir's inner elbow, and he gazed down at her with a hard expression. "You don't think..."

His lips twisted as he looked away from her, and his gaze turned vacant, but his head twitched in an imitation of a nod.

I think I knew what he was thinking.

That lab was long abandoned.

But what if it's the only option they have?

"I know where they've gone," Lanir grunted out, and Samara's gaze jerked to him as tears formed in her eyes.

"I don't want you to go back there."

Lanir seemed to ignore her words, but his shoulders tensed further. "You will not be coming with us."

Samara stared at him, her eyes flickering around his face as if she were trying to take in every micro-expression. After a pause, she nodded, even as her lip trembled. "I understand."

Ilk exchanged a look with Lanir. "Eldich, Vitri, you take Tegan and Samara back to my cave. *Secure* them inside."

"I don't want to be locked up again," Tegan interrupted, her expression somewhere between fear and determination as she stepped back away from us.

"It's okay," Samara whispered, placing a hand on

Tegan's shoulder and flinching as Tegan jerked from her touch.

Ryth approached Tegan, towering over her as she cowered. "We need to know you're safe."

"Why?" Tegan demanded, her eyes shimmering with tears.

Ryth's lip twitched. "Don't make me tie you up to keep you there."

Tegan glared at Ryth even as she took another step away from him. But after a pleading look from Samara, Tegan crossed her arms over her chest. "Fine."

"Carry them," Ilk commanded, pointing at Tegan and Samara. "Then meet us in the fields beyond my cave. Go."

I scowled at Ilk. His commanding tone would be easier to take seriously if my entire world wasn't falling around me at the thought of losing Amy. She was the only one in immediate danger, and with every passing second, there was more and more distance between us.

Tegan glanced uneasily at Vitri and the vines that wrapped around his arms and torso before she turned to me and allowed me to lift her on my back. Her small arms clung around my neck, and I supported her legs and tucked them around my forearms.

"Ready?" I asked, trying not to watch as Samara littered Lanir's face with kisses and whispered things in his ear as he snarled. She climbed onto Vitri's back, and tears shone in her eyes as she stared at Lanir as if she couldn't stand not to see him for even a second.

Tegan nodded against my shoulder, and I took off at a run.

CHAPTER 20

AMY

Every step was agony. Tori had started to stir in the past few minutes, and every movement she made tilted the stretcher painfully on my shoulders.

"Shh," I whispered to her, not even knowing if she could hear me. "It's okay. Just rest."

But it wasn't okay.

It was incredibly *far* from okay.

We hadn't stopped for a break, and aside from a hastily passed-around water bag where Misha and I had seconds to get a drink, we'd had nothing to eat, and the weakness was beginning to drag me down. The tunnel had started sloping upward, and this created a flush of conflicting feelings within me.

Relief because this part of the journey was almost over.

Fear because of what waited at the other end.

Resignation because I couldn't escape my fate with the Ghaal.

They hadn't stopped talking the entire way, and every conversation between them grew more aggressive in tone, even when I couldn't understand what was being said. Several fights had broken out, and as I grit my teeth, another fight started, and I forced myself not to look behind me. The last time their shouting increased, curiosity had gotten the better of me, and I'd turned to see what was happening, only to be rewarded with a slap that had almost knocked me to the ground.

The scuffling behind Misha and I increased in volume as two or more Ghaal fought. I clenched my jaw and focused on putting one foot in front of the other. I risked a sideways glance at Misha, and her eyes were wide with fear.

Something was going on, but we couldn't understand their language.

We were jerked to a stop when two Ghaal grabbed our arms and forced us to halt before they pointed angrily at the ground. "Stay still."

I turned to find four Ghaal fighting. One had his forearm wrapped around the throat of another, his legs around his torso as he choked him with his forearm, while two others scuffled either side as they tried to break them apart. The Ghaal being choked started clawing at the arm of the one holding him down, and just when I thought he was going to pass out, the Ghaal holding him stood and released his hold.

The Ghaal gasped for air, only to grab the side of his head and slammed into the tunnel wall.

The crunch of his skull breaking brought bile up my throat, and my eyes watered as I tried desperately to stop coughing and attracting attention to myself.

The body dropped to the ground, and blood leaked from his temple and ears before another explosion of shouts sounded out. I couldn't believe what I was seeing—even with so few of them left, they killed each other over arguments. When I quickly passed my eyes across the small gathering, I noticed several injuries and fresh blood that couldn't have been there when we entered the tunnel.

Putting the Ghaal in close quarters, they would almost take each other out.

Which would be a good thing if we weren't trapped in here with them.

While the fighting Ghaal were brought under control by others, the two who had stopped Misha and me from walking grabbed our arms again and began to tug us forward. They let us go the moment we moved on our own but stayed by our sides.

"It's too late for us," one of them said, and while I desperately wanted to know what the arguments had been about, I kept my head down and didn't engage. He was speaking so I could understand, and I had to be suspicious of his motivations. "We have no chance left. This is the end of the line."

"So, let us go," Misha ventured, and the two Ghaal flanking us laughed quietly.

"We have no means off this planet. Even if we *could* get the technology to fly, we'd be destroyed in the net around our atmosphere, stopping us from leaving. Our gestation period is six months, and *if* we manage to get you all pregnant, we can't keep the Synths away for that long."

I looked up to see Misha glaring at him. "Then why are we still here?"

"Ghaal are stubborn. We won't give up, even when all is lost... no technology, no escape, and nowhere to go. Hundreds of years of dwindling numbers, technology, and knowledge, hundreds of years of increased agitation and violent tendencies. We were doomed from the start."

"Kinda sounds like it was your own fault," Misha spat out, and my eyebrows shot up. I admired her bravery, but was this the time to be poking the proverbial bear?

"Even if we all die tomorrow, we'll make sure our bloodline lives on." He offered me a hard stare, and while I tried to hold it, I couldn't and looked at the ground again as he added, "In you all."

My legs collapsed as we exited the tunnel into the building. The only light source was the holes in the ceiling—the walls and roof rotted away from years of neglect. We must have been walking overnight. Although my sense of time was skewed, I'm certain it was afternoon when we left, and we'd been walking longer than the few hours it would've been until sunset.

I tried to ignore the sting in my shoulders, certain there were blisters under my clothes, as I lowered Tori on the stretcher gently to the floor and worked to undo her restraints. The Ghaal was fussing about the room, unpacking their bags and setting things up. Apart from a few who stood nearby to watch over us, they otherwise ignored us. Some lights flickered before going out again, and a dull electric hum sounded, followed by a spark and a smattering of angry chatter from the Ghaal.

Tori's eyes fluttered open as I leaned over her.

"Wh..." she started before she groaned and licked her lips. I had no water to offer her. "Where are we?"

"Just relax. You've been coming down from the drugs."

A smile tugged at her lips even as her eyes closed again. "Did we get them?"

I could hear the smirk in Misha's voice as she replied for me, "Oh yeah, you got them. You fucked them up good."

"So, we're safe?" When neither of us answered, Tori cracked an eye open and stared at me. I bit my bottom lip and shook my head before pressing a finger to my lips.

"Get her up," a Ghaal nearby snapped as he came closer.

"She's not recovered yet. The poison is still in her system," I said.

He stopped in his tracks and eyed me suspiciously before his gaze fell on Tori as she lay on the stretcher. Her chest rose and fell with a steady rhythm. He turned to his comrade. "How long does it last?"

"How am I supposed to know?" the other snapped.

They continued chatting in their language while I glanced over at Misha and indicated Erica with my chin. Misha nodded but said nothing. Okay, so both were awake, but as long as the Ghaal thought they were still poisonous, they were safe.

I hoped.

Misha was already pregnant, which means the

only one who was in immediate danger was—

I grunted as hands wrapped under my arms and forced me to my feet. I wanted to fight, but my legs were so weak, and my body drained of energy from the long walk carrying myself and Tori's weight with no food and little water. "This way."

Misha got to her feet and shoved at the Ghaal. "Get your hands off her."

He shoved back, and Misha lost her balance, tripped over Erica's legs, and landed hard on her ass. She glared up at the Ghaal as others came and dragged her to her feet.

"Restrain them."

"Okay, but I'm not touching those two."

The Ghaal eyed Erica and Tori as they lay on the floor, and there was an unspoken tension in the room. They knew it was the end of the line for them, but that didn't mean they weren't going to cling to their lives with every ounce of strength they had. One made a clicking sound with his tongue before he moved forward, grabbed Tori's upper arms, and held her tight for a few seconds. There was silence as the others watched him for a reaction, and he held his hands out, seeking the spotting of his skin that would indicate he had been poisoned.

Nothing.

He swept his hand through the air. "Restrain them *all.*"

Tori and Erica jumped to their feet and barreled

through the Ghaals. They had nowhere to go, but they ran anyway, even as the group closed in on them. The Ghaal who held me steered me away from the scene and toward the rear of the large room. I glanced up at the tall ceilings and let my gaze trace the vines that grew through the cracks in the wall and tangled themselves around the furniture and equipment left behind.

"What is this place?" I whispered, not expecting an answer.

"This is where the Synths were created."

I gasped before my lip trembled as thoughts of Eldich flooded my mind.

Will he come for me? Is he already on his way? Will he get here in time?

I was shoved onto a table, and when the Ghaal hovered his hand over a silver ball near it, a restraint clamped over my wrist. He frowned as the other restraints stayed still, and I took the opportunity to lurch my body over. I tried to roll off the table, but the angle of my restrained arm made it impossible, so I pulled at the restraint and tried to wiggle my hand free.

But it was too late.

Other Ghaal had gathered and used ropes to tie me down.

"We could only carry so much with us," one of them explained to me, and I fought against the binds, ignoring the way the rope chafed the soft skin on my neck as I was held down. "We can only do one of you at a time, but don't worry…" I jerked my head to the side as he brushed my hair from my face. "It won't take long. In fact, I think you might like it."

I wanted to spit in his face, but my mouth was dry. "Why the fuck would I *like* it? You're all disgusting."

"Because…" he leaned in close to my ear, and I shuddered as he played with the ropes that held me down, almost a sensual caress. "We had to leave most of our DNA reserves behind. The equipment was too much to carry, and the frozen samples wouldn't make the journey. But luckily, we have fresh samples…" I couldn't hold back the tears that blurred my vision, but the orange of his eyes was clear as he hovered over me. "Samples we scraped from your Synth after he spent the night with you in the cell."

I stilled.

Eldich's DNA?

So, the baby would be…

I shook my head vigorously and fought against the binds. I still didn't want this. I didn't want the Ghaal to touch me *at all.* The one above me sneered as those around him chuckled, and I wiggled as the ropes were tightened and my legs were spread. "Too bad we couldn't do it manually. We were going to give it a shot, but it might not take, and we don't have time to risk it." He tutted before he licked up the side of my face, tasting the tears on my skin. "Maybe we'll try it anyway after the procedure."

CHAPTER 21

ELDICH

Unleashing Lanir upon the remaining Ghaal would be like releasing an animal from his cage, and I wouldn't be far behind him. The time it had taken us to cover the ground to the abandoned lab had started with a churning of my stomach until my nerves practically vibrated with rage and need.

If the Ghaal wanted us to release the instinct within, then so be it.

I remembered this place, and all the memories I'd pushed so far down rushed back when we stood outside the building and stared at the decrepit exterior walls. The memories of the pain we suffered were so strong my knees almost buckled, and even Ilk and Ryth skidded to a stop next to me as we stared up at the twisted metal that made up what was once grand Ghaal architecture. This entire continent was once a bustling metropolis, but after the wars, it was all destroyed, and the remaining Ghaal retreated to a small colony by the ocean. Nature took over, and over the decades before we were even created, while the Ghaal struggled to solve their infertility issues caused by chemical warfare, the continent returned to its former glory before it was ever populated.

Now, the last Ghaal colony was destroyed, and they'd taken our mates here for their final stand.

But what if they weren't here?

Vitri and Ilk had spoken of a small base in the forest farther away where Erica had been taken once. She had only seen the cells, so she couldn't determine if a lab existed, but it was a possibility. This lab had long since been abandoned but had been stocked up with all the technology they needed. It was used for our creation and was intentionally situated away from the colony in case the experiment went wrong to reduce the risk of unnecessary casualties.

And it went wildly wrong when we decided we'd had enough of the torture, broke free, and killed anyone who stood in our way.

My hands shook as I remembered. I lifted them

and stared at my fingers as if expecting to see them once again caked with sticky blood. How many Ghaal had I killed with my bare hands? How many necks and backs had I broken in my desperation to escape this place and *live?* Killing for the sake of it wasn't in our nature—it was against everything we stood for.

But as much as we had backed the Ghaal into a corner with the execution of the plan earlier, they had also pushed us beyond the point of no return. The females deserved a life as much as we did, and the Ghaal would never stop. Once we crossed the threshold into the lab, there was no going back, and we would kill them all or die trying.

Ilk and I exchanged a glance, and while we didn't say anything, there was still something we hadn't discussed.

Would we kill them *all*, or would we offer them a chance to live on without disturbing us?

Who were we to make the ultimate decision to wipe a species from the face of the planet?

Although the Ghaal had nearly done that to themselves.

Was this something they had discussed at Ilk's without me?

These were not the last Ghaal in existence, though. Practically an entire generation had left almost a hundred years ago in search of another planet they could populate. Those who remained here were determined to save *this* home and were sure they could solve the issues that caused their dwindling numbers.

These Ghaal who were alive now were the children of the Ghaal who had remained on this planet, and their children's children. Knowledge of technology and its maintenance had been lost along with much of the history before the wars. More and more, they were turning to simpler, more natural living because they had no choice.

But they still didn't care for any living beings but themselves.

Vitri reached out to his side and grabbed Lanir's upper arm. He didn't flinch when Lanir rounded on him and snarled as his eyes flashed and pupils dilated. Lanir's mate was safe, but the emotions of the past few weeks had tightened inside him like a coil, exacerbated by being back at the place of his creation and the worst of his torture. Lanir was about to be released, and as much as I hated using his anger as fuel for the weapon he could be, we were going to point him straight at the Ghaal.

"Plan?" Vitri asked.

"Sol goes in with us, and we all have darts with eylak venom. Use it," Ilk answered.

"I'll collect and destroy any weapons I can find that can harm you," Sol added, and I glanced at him. We didn't know how many of the weapons they had left that could shut us down. It had been built into our DNA, and a swipe from the needle would be enough to get into our bloodstream and take out our organs one by one—a failsafe built into us. It did nothing to the Ghaal—their DNA didn't react to the formula. The ease with which we could be killed kept us from the Ghaal colony for too long, and I, along with my brothers, would have to live with the guilt that even though we spent our days saving all the species we could, we didn't do enough.

It was selfish and made my stomach churn more, but the knowledge that if we had risked our lives to take out the Ghaal years before, we would never have met our mates filled me with conflicting emotions. I didn't want the females to suffer, but I stood on the precipice of a future with Amy.

The Ghaal had instilled a great deal of terror in us through torture, and even being back here made my skin crawl. I glanced at Lanir, and his lip was lifted into a constant snarl, but his eyes darted around as if looking for an escape from this place.

None of us wanted to be here, but this had to end *now*.

"This is war," Sahcor said without turning around. "We've been tactical, and now it's time to be brutal. Surround, overcome, kill. There's nothing else to it."

I straightened my spine, needing only one thought to keep me moving forward into this building and push aside the memories that lived here.

Amy needs me.

Vitri slowly removed his hand from Lanir's arm. "Now."

AMY

When there was an explosion of sound, I didn't move and instead remained curled up in the fetal position in the corner of the room. I'd shuffled behind some of the abandoned tables and equipment, unable to face the other girls after the procedure. There was lingering pain, but nothing I couldn't handle, but the discomfort was worse if I moved. I didn't remember much—either I passed out, or they gave me something. The entire event was hazy. But I knew what they'd done, and it was enough to send me inside myself, needing to hide from everything. So even with my arms tied behind my back and my legs bound, once the Ghaal dumped me near the other girls, I hadn't settled until I'd shuffled myself into a corner. When I looked up as I was moving across the cold floor, Misha caught my eye. The distress in her gaze didn't make my pain any easier, so I looked away.

The Ghaal shouted, and footsteps pounded across the floor around the corner from where I hid.

I could hear Misha's muffled shouts behind her gag.

They'd come for us.

But they were too late.

Tori had been dragged off shortly after I was dumped in the corner with the others, tied up and gagged. It only felt like minutes ago, but maybe it was hours. I couldn't tell anymore. Perhaps the Ghaal hadn't performed the procedure on her yet.

I didn't want anyone else to feel what I was feeling.

The floor trembled after it sounded like a wall had collapsed, and the roar of one of the Synths made me flinch. *Who was that? Is that Eldich?* It didn't sound like him and could be one of the brothers. But then again, when he'd been tortured and thrown into the cell with me, he'd turned animal, and his voice became gravelly and dark.

"Amy!" I heard Eldich cry out for me.

Answer him, my mind screamed at me. *Get out of your hiding place and find him!*

But I couldn't find it in myself to move.

So I tucked further into a ball and pressed my cheek against the cold floor.

A bunch of bones breaking sounded too close to me for comfort. A splatter of blood hit the table I hid behind, and some of it splashed onto my forehead. I flinched again as the tears started.

"Eldich..." I whimpered, but the sound behind the gag was muffled, and how could he hear me over the chaos anyway? Screaming, roaring, and running filled the room. Every now and then, the sounds would be punctuated by the thud of a body hitting the floor, and I could only squeeze my eyes shut and hope it wasn't a Synth or one of the girls.

"Amy!" Eldich's desperate cry was closer now, and this time, I found my voice and tried to scream behind the gag as I shuffled my way across the floor. I screamed again when something shot past my head and hit the floor behind me with a metallic clang. I couldn't see what it was, and not knowing if I was being attacked or rescued made me freeze. My mind blanked, unsure what to do or where to go. Misha and Erica were nowhere to be seen.

When I looked up, I screamed into the gag.

A demon stood over me—his skin a deep ash gray with lines of orange like it was cracked and showing hellfire beneath. He tilted his head before he reached down and grabbed me, and I wiggled in my restraints as I tried to kick him when he threw me over his shoulder. The demon ran into the chaos, and I could barely see what was happening as I bounced on his shoulder. There were bodies everywhere, the floor was covered in gray blood, and the metallic smell stung my nose. I mumbled Eldich's name behind my gag, but the demon didn't stop even as I sobbed.

"Amy..." The relief in Eldich's voice brought on a new wave of sobs from me, and they grew heavier

as the demon lifted me off his shoulder and handed me to Eldich. I shook my head and squeezed my eyes shut as tears blurred my vision. I wanted to apologize to the demon-looking alien for misjudging him. Apparently, he was another Synth, and I wanted to thank him. But he'd already turned and run back into the battle, picked up a Ghaal as he passed, brought the alien down over his knee, and broke his spine without the slightest bit of hesitation.

I screamed at the display of violence and turned my head toward Eldich's chest as he worked to undo my ties with one hand while he held me close with the other.

"It's okay, Amy. It's okay. You're safe now, I promise." He placed me on my feet and backed us away to the side of the room as he ran his hands up and down my arms. I wanted to tell him what had happened to me, what they had done, but every time I opened my mouth, only a sob would escape, and Eldich would shush me gently.

A Ghaal holding something small in his hand ran toward Eldich while he was fussing with me.

"Look out!" I cried, and Eldich jerked to the side as the Ghaal reached out to swipe him. The Ghaal missed, spun under his own momentum, and when he turned to try again, another Synth was behind him—Sahcor—grabbed his arm and shoulder and broke the limb almost off. The Ghaal screamed and dropped to his knees as the bone protruded, and the weapon he was holding clattered to the floor.

Sahcor stared at it and slowly raised his eyes to Eldich. "He didn't get you, did he?"

Eldich shook his head.

Then his arm jerked, and he dropped to one knee and clutched his leg.

"*No,*" Sahcor cried. He leaped at Eldich and held his shoulders as he lowered him into a lying position.

Eldich's limbs began jerking, but his eyes were on me.

"What's happening?" I screamed as I fell to my knees next to Sahcor and placed my hands on Eldich's arm. "What did they do to him?"

Sahcor was trembling. "We were designed with a failsafe, and the Ghaal have a weapon they can use to shut us down. Only the smallest cut—"

"No." I refused to accept this and shuffled along until Sahcor was forced to move out of the way as I lifted Eldich's arm. He still wasn't speaking, but his eyes were following every movement I made. "No, it barely touched him. There isn't even a cut here, no blood."

"It touched his skin. It's all it needed. It'll just take longer now."

"No, no, *no, no, no.* Eldich, *please.* Please don't die." My crying had attracted another Synth's attention, and I didn't bother to turn around to look at him as I saw the dappled gray feet stop next to where I kneeled.

"Ilk," Sahcor said, looking up at his brother over my shoulder as I bawled. "What can we do?"

"There's nothing we can do."

I threw my head back and screamed, a wordless sound drawn from the agony that opened up inside my chest.

We didn't have enough time together.

We were meant to escape and be *together.*

"Eldich," I whispered and leaned down before I kissed him on the forehead. "Can you hear me?" He blinked, his head jerked, and his fingers twitched where I held his hand. I chose to believe that was a yes, and it wasn't over for us yet.

The sounds of the fights behind me meant nothing now—all my focus was on Eldich.

"Please don't die. We were going to live together, remember? You and me together. You promised." It sounded so childish, pleading for him not to die, but I didn't know what else to do. I couldn't accept there was *nothing* that could be done, but my mind was blank when I tried to think of any action I could take.

A tear slid down Eldich's cheek, and I sobbed loudly. I was being selfish. If these were his last moments, he didn't need to be reminded of all the things he wasn't going to have. I could grieve later, lock myself away, and suffer alone. But right now,

Eldich needed *me.*

"You saved me," I whispered before another sob lurched from my throat as he jerked again. This time, the jerk of his limbs started a chain reaction until he was having a seizure. I tried to hold his face as he moved. "You saved me. You saved me, and I love you."

The battle behind me faded into nothing, and all I could do was cry while I watched Eldich slowly die in front of me.

AMY

"Move!"

I screamed as I was shoved to the side by a Ghaal and began attacking him when he reached for Eldich. "Don't touch him. Don't you touch him!"

Sahcor grabbed my arms and pulled me back, but I fought his hold and struggled even as he crossed my arms over my chest, wrapped his arms around me, and held me still while the Ghaal moved over Eldich. "Shh," Sahcor whispered as he tucked his head next to mine and rested his chin on my shoulder. "He's with us."

"Sol," Ilk's heavy voice rumbled behind me.

There was a break in his voice, and I shuddered with another sob. These were Eldich's family—his brothers. This wasn't just about me, but I couldn't still myself in Sahcor's arms. I needed to be near my mate. "What are you doing?"

Sol drove a needle into Eldich's arm, as Eldich's eyes rolled back in his head. "Everything I can," he answered before he turned to Sahcor. "Hold this needle in place, and don't let it go."

Sahcor released me, and I immediately shuffled across the floor to the other side of Eldich's body while Sahcor clamped his arm. While Eldich jerked and flailed, the needle kept moving, and Sol muttered under his breath. Ilk came forward, straddled Eldich's legs, and pressed his large hands onto his shoulders, holding Eldich still. I watched with wide eyes as Sol set up some equipment before digging into his skin with a needle. Precious seconds passed before the gray of his blood flowed through a tube and began to drip into Eldich's arm.

"What are you doing?" I asked.

Sol looked up at me. "The weapon only works on Synth DNA. Ghaal DNA is immune. If I can get enough of my blood into his system, I might be able to stop it from killing him."

"But..." I licked my lips, tasting the salt from my tears. "Won't losing that much blood kill you?"

Sol didn't look at me again, his focus on the needle in Eldich's arm. "Most definitely."

The seconds turned into minutes, and I watched Eldich carefully as Sol's blood was delivered into his body. When he stopped flailing around, I released an unsteady breath and leaned down to kiss his clammy forehead. "It's going to be okay, baby," I whispered against his damp skin covered in a sheen of sweat. "It's all going to be okay." I wanted desperately to believe my words, but all I had to go on was the word of a *Ghaal,* and how could I trust him? No matter what he was doing to help now, did that change what he had done before?

I glanced between Eldich's two brothers, and their eyes were fixated on Sol as well.

We waited.

There was a scuffle from behind Sahcor, but I didn't bother looking up, and it was subdued after a snarling and snapping sound, followed by a scream of pain. The voice in pain was twisted with a strange quality to it that the Ghaal had.

It wasn't a Synth hurt or one of the girls, therefore I didn't care.

Eldich's skin started changing, the white tint amongst the pale yellow getting a gray tinge to it. His eyes moved rapidly behind his closed eyelids, and his fingers twitched where I held his hand.

"Eldich?" I whispered.

He didn't respond.

The changes were so slow they were almost undetectable, but Eldich *was* changing. His skin became grayer, and the roots of his hair darkened to a deeper purple. The shape of his face stayed the same, and I was grateful that whatever was happening, it wouldn't take away who Eldich was fundamentally.

"Sol," I choked out his name, and when he looked up at me, his movements were weak and slow. His face was pale and covered in sweat, and his hand trembled where he held the needle against his arm. "What's happening?"

"It's working," was all he managed, and my eyes widened as I looked back down at Eldich before directing my attention to Sahcor. I wanted to understand, and Sahcor met my eyes and nodded.

"The Synth DNA allows us to adapt to our environment. But as that's being overcome with the Ghaal blood, it's fighting the poison, but it's also returning him to our original form."

"So, he'll look like…" I swallowed, and my gaze darted back to Eldich, "… a Ghaal?"

Sahcor's gaze was unreadable. "Not quite. They didn't want us to be too like them. But he'll be closer than he is now." He adjusted where his hands were around Eldich's arm, holding the needle. "We can't know for sure. We've never done this before."

My teeth worked over my bottom lip as I tried to understand. Then my gaze fell to the steady flow of blood from Sol to Eldich. "It's too much extra blood.

It'll kill him." I couldn't help the sharp edge to my voice.

Sol shook his head slowly as though the motion took all his strength. "He's an engineered being. His blood will absorb and merge with mine. His body will adapt."

The sounds around me faded until I was almost convinced I could hear the flow of blood from one being to another.

"Sahcor…" Sol's voice was weak, and Sahcor reached out an arm just as the Ghaal collapsed. Sahcor helped ease him to the floor, and Sol blinked up at him as Misha kneeled beside him. "All of it, give him… all the blood."

"You're dying," Sahcor said. I couldn't read any emotion in his voice, but something flickered across his eyes as he watched the dying Ghaal by his side.

Sol simply smiled up at him before he looked at Misha. "Make it fast. Death from blood loss is painful."

Misha's brows were pulled together even as her eyes shimmered with what could be tears. The internal battle she was facing was breaking her apart, and to a point I could understand. I didn't know the history between Misha and Sol or what she'd been through before I was woken from my sleep chamber.

But there was definitely history there, even though he was a Ghaal.

Did she offer him mercy at his time of death?

"Thank you for all you've done." She reached out to brush Sol's face, but instead, her hand hovered over his skin without making contact.

"The very least…" he whispered back.

"Do it," Misha whispered to Sahcor.

Misha swiped a hand across her face as she switched places with Sahcor and took hold of Eldich's arm. Sahcor rested Sol's head in his lap. Sol looked up at him, and a small smile played on his face. "You really are… our greatest creation."

When Sol started to jerk around, his body going into shock at the loss of blood, Sahcor placed his hands around Sol's head…

Before he snapped his neck.

Sol's body went limp, and Sahcor shifted him to make sure the rest of his blood would be transferred to Eldich. I intertwined my fingers with Eldich's and gasped when I realized his fingers were no longer elongated. A quick look showed his toes were shorter, too, and more in scale with his feet. His skin had almost completely grayed and had a dappling of a strange texture on it.

But his face—I brushed it with my fingers and cupped his cheek in my palm—*is still Eldich.*

"He'll live." I glanced up at Ilk as he stood from where he'd been restraining Eldich and held his hand out to me. "We have one last task here."

There were six Ghaal left.

Ironic it was six, considering in their last moments they had abandoned their faith in the number. If I were superstitious or religious, I might think it was a cruel punishment for them. Six of them were left on the planet to remind them of the beliefs they once held and how forsaking them had apparently cost them their lives.

The girls and I gathered near each other, touching arms and faces and embracing, unable to speak, for what was there to say? Every few seconds, I would glance nervously back at where Eldich lay, but he was breathing steadily, his body healing, I supposed, figuring itself out with the new blood. Designed to not only survive but to thrive. He was strong and created to be the best. I clung to that in my mind with everything I had, even as Erica introduced me to the other Synths. I nodded, and each time had offered my name in a small voice, but I'd suddenly found myself drained of energy. Yet, at the same time, there was lingering anxiety in my gut, as if my body was ready to fight or run again at any second.

I couldn't quite believe our ordeal was over.

The lab was littered with Ghaal bodies, some of

them broken nearly in half, others with their chest or guts ripped out, but most with their heads twisted at odd angles as their necks had been broken. The Synths had come through this room like a fucking tornado and simply ripped the Ghaal to shreds.

All except these six in front of me.

All males.

They were tied back-to-back, sitting in a small circle in the middle of the lab as Ilk crouched down in front of them and studied them. The Ghaal glared at him but said nothing.

"You have a choice," Ilk started, only for the Ghaal in front of him to spit at his feet. The Ghaal hissed something at him in their strange language, and Ilk simply tilted his head. "No. No native language. The females deserve to hear this." He watched the Ghaal in front of him for a beat longer before he continued, "Wiping a species from a planet is not something I wanted to do, but you've forced our hand."

"Let's kill them." Lanir snarled.

"Wait," Erica's voice shook as she spoke up and moved to place a hand on Lanir's arm, stopping just short of contact. "I know what they've done. Please believe me when I say I understand, Lanir. But to make an entire species extinct? Who are we to take that responsibility?"

"They did it to themselves," Lanir grunted out,

and I quietly agreed.

"They won't be extinct," Sahcor added, looking at Erica. "Most of them left the planet to try to find a home elsewhere and hope of breeding. For all we know, there could be an entire planet full of them somewhere." He turned to the Ghaal in front of him, who, despite their situation, didn't look afraid and continued to glare at the Synths. "So, the question is purely why should these ones be allowed to live?"

"Ilk," Erica whispered and waited until he glanced at her. "Make them the offer."

Ilk looked at Erica, and after she nodded again, he turned back to the Ghaal in front of him. "Here is our offer. We will destroy all your remaining technology and give you the chance to live a life away from us. To live off the land."

"What kind of life is that?" one of the Ghaal spat out and bared his teeth at Ilk. "To live like *savages?*"

"It's more life than you deserve," Ilk snarled at the Ghaal and bared his teeth in return.

"We'll never stop."

"Why?" Tori cried out and stepped forward as she threw her arms in the air. Her eyes shimmered with angry tears, and her cheeks flushed as a deep furrow formed between her brows. "It's over! You've lost. We're offering you a chance to live out your lives in peace, something you never offered us."

The Ghaal closest to her surged forward, the

others shifting with him as he attempted to lunge at Tori. Tori gasped as she spun away and rubbed her arms as though her skin were crawling. Her fear of the Ghaal was like mine, running so deep that even their being tied up and subdued was not enough to feel safe around them. But I understood Erica's hesitation—taking a life was not something to be done lightly, and this was an entirely new level, wiping an entire species from the face of the planet. Even though the Ghaal had proven themselves not worth saving, uneasiness still settled over us as we watched them on the floor. Offering them *one last chance* seemed to be the thing we needed to do to save our sanity.

Because in order to do this and not be haunted by it, we had to at least try. Right?

Ilk roared at the one who'd lunged at Tori, grabbed his shoulder and head, and twisted until the crunch of a breaking neck that was becoming all too familiar to me echoed around the room. I winced and took another step back from the Ghaal.

I didn't want to be here.

I wanted this to be over.

I wanted it to be over without having to be the one to *make sure* it was over.

I glanced around the group of Synths. Four of them were standing tall around the Ghaal with Ilk kneeling in front of them, while the other women and I hovered further back, no one looking anywhere near relaxed. We were putting a lot onto the Synths' shoulders. They'd taken it upon themselves to protect and care for us and, from what I'd heard, welcomed the girls into their homes.

Cared for us.

Loved us.

I looked back at Eldich again, and my hands gripped and released by my sides. He was still breathing a slow, steady rhythm that helped me to settle.

He was going to be okay.

He *was* okay.

Sol's lifeless body lay next to Eldich, the blood no longer flowing, and Sahcor had removed the needle from Eldich's arm before he stepped away.

The Synths had waited until we were all here to help make this choice.

A shuffle caught my eye, and I turned to see Erica with her head bowed as she muttered something I couldn't hear.

Misha clung to Sahcor as his palm rested on her stomach. I almost smiled. I guess he finally knew about her pregnancy. That was good—I wanted them to be happy.

Blinking a few times, I dragged my thoughts back to the present moment. "What do we do?" I whispered to no one in particular. I made eye contact with each of the women in turn and nodded to myself when no one answered.

We all knew how this was going to end.

"You can wait outside," Vitri offered, and I almost laughed. Like we hadn't already seen enough chaos and violence to last a lifetime, he was offering us an out not to witness this final act.

"No," I said, surprised to hear how steady my voice was. These were the beings who had ordered my abduction, killed my friends, and tortured Eldich and me.

Almost *killed* Eldich and nearly took him from me before we even had a chance to really be together.

Killed Becca.

If this was going to end, I needed to see it.

One of the Ghaal looked at me, a sneer visible through where blood ran from his nose. "You will carry on our legacy," he said.

I recoiled and stepped back as my lip trembled. Erica came up next to me and placed her palm on my lower back. Her presence was comforting. I didn't know much about her, but she felt like a mother-hen type, and I took the comfort I was offered and leaned into her.

"Do it," she said.

Lanir roared again, and I jumped back as he lunged at the group. He grabbed two of the remaining five Ghaal and squeezed their heads with his thumbs in their eye sockets as they screamed before he slammed their faces together. Ilk, Sahcor, and Vitri broke the necks of the others, a quick death perhaps they didn't deserve, but it was enough to keep what was left of my conscience.

I sighed loudly as the last Ghaal body hit the floor, and together, we stood in silence, knowing the Ghaal would never be a threat to us again.

The sound of the wind blowing through the holes in the walls and ceiling moved past me, and I took a deep, steadying breath. The cool air felt like my first breath of freedom in a long time.

We may have been taken from our homes, but we had the chance to start a new life here without the danger.

It was finally over.

CHAPTER 23

ELDICH

Groaning, I lifted an arm to my forehead and moaned again when the movement felt like more work than I had the energy for. When I tried to open my eyes, dots of light danced across my vision, and I closed them again. Wherever I was, it wasn't too bright, but the mere act of opening my eyes had caused a rush to my head. I adjusted myself where I lay, pressed my hands down by my sides, and felt the soft furs beneath me.

I was in somebody's bed.

Am I home?

Where is Amy?

That second thought had me sitting bolt upright, only to be rewarded with a strong rush to my head that had me swaying. Blinking through the discomfort, I focused on my hands, crying out when they came into focus.

"Wha…" My skin wasn't my own. Gone were the soft colors of the woodlands I had been living in with the sandy soil, as well as the length of my fingers that helped move through the trees. My skin was gray now, and my fingers were thicker and slightly shorter. I turned my hands over and bit my lower lip against the emotion that threatened to surface as I saw the texture of scales running up my wrist. Ghaal didn't have true scales, but the pattern was a long-lost ancestral trait that never left even as they evolved.

With a surge of panic, I reached behind me and ran my hands over my shoulders. They were smooth with no tufts of thick purple hair. I released a shaky sigh. So, I didn't appear like a full Ghaal but had, for some reason, returned to my original form—looking like a simplified Ghaal, ready to be molded.

Which I suppose was what they wanted when they created us.

Where is Amy?

"Amy?" I tried to shout, but my voice croaked out into nothing. I reached out and felt the furs and rocks around me, seeking a water bag. When I found it, I brought it to my lips and gulped down gratefully. "Amy!" I cried out, and relief flooded me when my voice still sounded like my own without the grating edge the Ghaal had. I slumped back in the bed as the lightheadedness returned, and closed my eyes. Pounding footsteps followed shortly, and a scraping sound could be heard before the soft panting of a woman echoed around the space.

"Eldich?" Amy's voice was like music to me, and I cracked open a single eye. With a cry, she dropped to her knees beside where I lay and ran her hands over my face, neck, shoulders, and chest as if feeling to see if I were real. I almost smiled and let her touch me—Amy could touch me all she wanted. "I knew I heard you call for me. Eldich? Can you hear me?"

"I can hear you, my mate," I mumbled.

She released a squeal and grabbed my face in her hands before she pressed her lips against mine. "You're okay. Thank God you're okay," she muttered against my lips as she kept pressing hers to my face, and I moaned at the sensation. She giggled then, and I felt weightless at that moment, hearing her happy. "The other girls told me Synths don't kiss," she said as she kept putting her lips against mine. This time, I pouted my lips, mimicking her, but was too late, as she had already pulled away. She chuckled again. "We have all the time in the world to kiss."

"Kiss," I whispered, closed my eyes, and pouted my lips again. Amy laughed quietly as she kissed me again—once, twice, three quick kisses that left me wanting more. Her lips were so soft, and they molded against mine. As she settled down, I shifted to the side so she could lie next to me and tucked an arm around her body while she placed her cheek in the crook of my shoulder and arm. "What happened?" I croaked out.

Amy tensed beside me, and I wanted to retract the question. She'd been through so much—too much because of the Ghaal. But I didn't understand where we were or why I looked like this. "After you and your brothers stormed the lab, there was a huge fight. One of the Ghaal got you with that little weapon they had against you." She took a deep breath as if preparing herself to say the words aloud. "You were dying."

She choked back a sob and then tucked herself further against me as her small hand curled against my chest. "I'm okay now," I mumbled as I ran my hand over her back.

"I know," she whispered, kissing my chest. "There was a Ghaal, Sol, who helped. He did a blood transfusion in the hopes his Ghaal DNA would reduce the effect of the weapon on your Synth DNA. Or something like that."

My brows drew together, but I kept my eyes closed. The amount of blood needed for something like that would have been high. "Sol?" I asked.

"He died," she said.

I nodded. Sol sacrificed his life to save me. "The Ghaal?"

"Gone. All of them are dead."

A growl rumbled through my chest, and although I hated the part of me that responded, my first thought had been *I wish I'd been there.* Instead, I was lying unconscious somewhere while my brothers took care of the last few Ghaal. I remembered we'd killed almost all of them when we'd stormed the lab. There was only one thing on my mind—*finding Amy*—and until that happened, I let out the animal the Ghaal had been trying to draw out of me for days. Bones snapped, and flesh was torn under my bare hands. While it wasn't a feeling I enjoyed, there was justice in the act.

"We're at Ilk's," Amy continued before I could ask. "We've been here for a couple of days. We haven't really spoken yet about the plan going forward. If we're all going to live here or..." she trailed off, and I stilled, waiting for her to continue. "Anyway, we wanted you to be part of the conversation, so we waited."

"How do you feel?" I asked as I finally opened my eyes and turned my head to face her. My vision was clearer now, and I took Amy in. Her hair was tied up on top of her head with a leather tie and secured in a little ball, and she wore a tunic and pants, teal green in color. I assumed Ilk had made them for her.

"Me?" she said as if she hadn't even considered herself in this equation. But knowing Amy as I knew her, she probably hadn't. I could almost picture her rushing between the other females and wanting to make sure they were okay—Tegan especially seemed to need some extra care—without taking a break to think of herself. "I'm good... I think. It's hard to wrap my head around everything, you know? The Ghaal is gone, and that in itself is weird. I'm surrounded by alien men who are more than capable of violence, and yet, I feel safe. I've got a group of women around me, and we've been getting to know each other. It's been... nice. In a weird way. There's this sense of peace now like we have no rush and nowhere to be, and we can simply take our time and enjoy life and being together." She looked into my eyes as she smiled. "But it's you I've been wanting to spend time with."

"Amy," I said, and her eyes brightened as she smiled more. "What color are my eyes?"

She furrowed her brows, the question confusing her. "Green. They've always been green, haven't they?"

I sighed, thankful they hadn't changed into the orange of the Ghaal. I didn't want Amy to be reminded of them every time she looked at me. "I have changed," I said simply.

"I know. Your body reacted to the Ghaal DNA. I

don't really understand it."

"If you no longer want to be with me, I will understand."

Amy sat up next to me and pressed a hand to my chest. I held her eye contact as she looked sternly down at me. "Don't ever think something like that. What kind of person would I be if I judged you for how you looked? And for something so completely out of your control?" Her eyes dropped, and her voice lowered. "And for something that saved your life when I thought I had lost you."

I pushed myself into a sitting position, wrapped an arm around Amy's waist, and pulled her against me. "I'm sorry for everything you went through."

"It's okay," she said before she made a small scoffing sound. *We both knew it was far from okay.* "We're here now, and I have you."

I leaned forward and inhaled her scent as I brushed my lips along her collarbone. "You still want me?" I questioned. I almost didn't dare to ask, but with the tremble of her in my arms, the memories of everything that had been, and how close we came to losing each other, I needed her now more than ever.

"Yes, definitely."

Amy giggled and squirmed as I licked along her neck, ending near her ear, where I gently sucked on her lobe with the odd hole for hanging decorations. Amy moaned and gripped my shoulders. My fingers found the edge of her pants, and I started tugging at them. "I need you naked."

Without hesitation, she stood and pressed a hand to my chest to guide me to stay down. She jogged over the entrance to Ilk's cave and pushed a light screen in front of the exit. The room was then bathed in a low light from the sunlight that seeped through the gaps around the screen. My pupils dilated as I adjusted to the lower light, and my jaw tensed as Amy stood in front of me and pulled her tunic over her head. She had a strap of fabric around her chest and held my eye contact while she undid the knot under her breasts and slowly unraveled the fabric before she dropped it to the cave floor. I couldn't keep looking at her eyes when the lure of her body was too much, and I took in the generous curve of her breasts and the swell of her stomach, creating a roll of sensual flesh. I wanted to feel every part of her, and when I reached out, she stepped back, giggling as I frowned.

"Like what you see?" She smiled.

"Very much. Come here." My voice was gravelly again, and the growl had returned to my chest, louder and more insistent than before. Amy had no hesitation, and there was no time to waste. We had both waited too long, and I needed to sink my cock into her waiting cunt more than I needed to breathe.

She shushed me gently and shimmed out of her

pants before she kicked them away. My gaze dropped to the tuft of hair she had between her legs and the flesh of her thighs. Her thighs touched between her legs, and my mouth watered as I imagined how she would feel around me.

How she would taste.

Slowly, she sauntered over toward me, and as soon as she was within my reach, I grabbed her and pulled her on my lap so she was straddling my legs. She squealed and laughed, the sound turning into a desperate moan as my mouth found her nipple. I sucked on her breast before moving to the other one, loving how she gasped and squirmed under my touch.

But then her body tensed, and I stopped my ministrations and pulled my mouth away slowly. While Amy still looked at me, her expression had become vacant as her eyes glazed over. "There something I have to tell you, Eldich, before we…"

"You can tell me anything. Nothing will make me want you less."

She nodded, but the graze of her teeth along her bottom lip told me she didn't believe me. "Before you came to rescue me, the Ghaal were… impatient." She whimpered as my fingers gripped her back, and I forced my body to relax, even though I felt I knew what was coming. "They wanted to impregnate us immediately before they even finished setting up the lab. They chose me…"

"Amy…" The idea of the Ghaal's hands on her sent a surge of rage through my body that was almost blinding. I would *never* blame Amy or hate her for what they had done, but the idea she thought less of herself because of it only made me want to prove to her otherwise.

I glanced at my arms and shuddered. How could she even stand to have me touch her when I look like this? Would I ever change again? What if I'd lost the ability to adapt? It seemed likely the Ghaal couldn't, and with the extra Ghaal blood in my system…

"They had some of your… stuff. Your sperm," she added when I looked confused. "They'd collected it from you after our second night together. They used it…"

"Amy… I'm so sorry."

"It's okay. I mean, I think I passed out for a moment. I don't remember the actual… procedure. But if it worked, and I'm carrying a baby, it's yours, right?" Before I could answer, she had started trembling and was biting her lip so hard I was afraid she might draw blood. "It's only been a few days. But I haven't been sick, and I'm not showing." She chuckled hollowly as she looked down and grabbed at her stomach. "Not that you'd be able to tell so soon."

"Amy—"

"I just didn't want you to hate me. Because if I *am*

pregnant, I don't want you to feel trapped like you're responsible even though you didn't do it just because it's yours biologically. I—"

"Amy," I grabbed her cheeks in my palms and used my thumb to wipe away a stray tear. "Nothing you say could ever make me want you less."

"But the baby—"

"The pregnancy may or may not have taken, we don't know. If you aren't, then that only gives me more time to make you mine. If you are, then that makes me happy, too, because nothing would complete me more than having a family with you."

"You mean it?"

"Yes. Are you okay?"

She stared at me for a moment. "I think so."

I didn't quite believe her. But how could she be? We looked at each other in silence for a few moments, and the feel of her skin next to mine was a comfort when I felt I needed her to be as close as possible.

"I mean..." she continued before I could speak, and I waited. "I'm not saying I haven't had my moments these past few days. I've cried a few times."

"Amy..." My chest constricted. *Again, she needed me, and I wasn't there.*

"But it's yours. Please tell me it's yours."

"It's mine. You're mine." Amy sighed and leaned

into my embrace. "I need you to answer something for me," I said.

"Anything," she whispered.

"Do I disgust you? Looking like *them*?"

"You're not *them*." She pulled away slightly so she could kiss my lips, moving away quickly before I could react. "You're you, and it's you I want."

"Do you want me to touch you now?" My mind blanked for a moment when she trembled, and her cheeks flushed. "Do you want me to fuck you, my mate?"

I had to be sure.

She'd been through so much.

Amy trembled again. This time, I could smell her need between us, and my pheromones increased in response. "Yes. *Please.*"

With a growl, I rolled over, lifted her with me, and lay her underneath me. Amy squealed with delight and chuckled. I smiled down at her and braced myself over her body. I wiped away another tear from her cheek. "No need to cry, Amy. It's all over, and I'll never let you go again."

"I like that you can lift me so easily," she muttered.

My eyebrows rose. "Of course, you're so small."

She laughed and reached up for me. "Come here and fuck me already."

When I pulled away, she frowned, but the expression eased as she moaned when I kissed my way down her body. "Soon, my mate, but first, I need to taste your cunt."

245

CHAPTER
24

AMY

When I reached over my head and gripped my fingers into the fur blankets, I arched my back and squeezed my eyes shut as I moaned. Eldich's face was between my legs, and he gripped my thighs tightly as he laved my pussy with enthusiasm. Long, languid licks from my ass to my clit were soon replaced with frantic lapping at my hole, and I cried out when he pressed his tongue inside me, and the thick muscle swirled inside my pussy.

"Fuck, Eldich, that feels so good…"

He simply hummed against me as his fingers tightened their grip and he pulled my legs farther apart to get in deeper.

"Fuck!" I reached forward, grabbed his head, and ground my pussy against his face. I was *aching* to come. Everything over the past few weeks, months, and *years* had been a nightmare. Eldich was the light at the end of the tunnel, and I wanted him more with every moment I spent with him. Almost losing him had created an ache in my heart that was beyond emotional. It was physical pain, and I could barely summon a smile for the other girls when they tried to cheer me up.

I'd thank them later for all their support, but right now, all I needed was this alien man between my legs.

"My clit, Eldich..." I panted and rubbed my clit with eager fingers. His bright green eyes watched the movement even as he kept his tongue buried inside me until he moved my hand out of the way with his chin and licked hungrily at my clit. The pressure and texture of his tongue was almost too much, and I screamed as I came, tilted my head back, and gripped his hair to hold him in place. The growling that rumbled from his chest started again, loud and dominating the space between us. When Eldich pulled away, I collapsed onto the furs even as I reached out for him.

"Please," I whispered as I grabbed his upper arms and pulled him so he was on top of me. "Please fuck me."

"You're so tight, my mate," he muttered, the growl heavy in his voice sent shudders through my body. When he lay on top of me between my spread legs, I could feel the vibrations through his chest, and my nipples hardened. I don't think I've ever been so turned on in my life, and the fact it was for an *alien* man while I currently lay in a cave on some strange planet almost had me laughing.

Until the feel of the head of his cock pressing against my pussy drove all other thoughts from my mind.

Eldich rocked his hips, and when his cock penetrated me, I cried out, and my fingers curled around his biceps. He snarled, and I forced myself to keep my eyes open, intent on watching his face as he sunk into me. My legs shook as he pushed in further, and the stretch of his large cock sent jolts of pleasure through my body. Eldich's eyes were closed in ecstasy as he bottomed out inside me, and I squirmed and writhed underneath him. My body was on the edge of another orgasm, and I barely had time to contemplate it when he thrust into me, and I came hard. Eldich silenced my cries by pressing his lips to mine, his body trembling above me as he began to gently thrust.

"You squeezed me so tight when you came, Amy..." his voice shuddered, and the muscles in his jaw and arms were taut as he tried to keep control. "If you do that again, I might not be able to hold back."

"Open your mouth," I whispered against his lips.

He complied, and I grabbed his face and pushed my tongue into his mouth. His resulting groan made me smirk until he took control and pressed his tongue forward. The taste of my release was all over his mouth, and we groaned together as he picked up the pace and fucked me harder. I spread my legs, opening myself up to him and moaning nonsensical praises as he fucked me into the bedding.

I'd never had unprotected sex before, but I wanted it with Eldich. If I were going to have a baby with him, I wanted it to be on our terms and not because we'd been forced. I wanted his cum to fill me because then I'd never have to think about the procedure again. If I got pregnant, it would be because of *this,* and nothing else that had happened mattered.

I chuckled when I realized I was completely okay with having a baby with someone I'd only just met. Eldich caught my smirk and lifted a questioning eyebrow at me. I raised my head to kiss his lips again before I pulled him closer to me and wrapped my arms around his shoulders.

"Come inside me, Eldich," I muttered.

He groaned again, and the rumble of his growl got louder. "I don't want it to end so soon."

"It's okay..." I ran my tongue along the skin under

his ear. "We have all the time we want."

"I hope you mean that, my mate." I cried out as he thrust *hard* into me a handful of times, keeping a grip on his shoulders to stop myself from shifting upward. "Because I'll never tire of fucking you."

"P-please…" I wasn't even sure what I was begging for, and my eyes rolled back as he hammered into me, his hips snapping against mine, each thrust stretching me open for him. Eldich raised himself so he could plant his hands on either side of my head, and I looked down to watch his large gray cock sink into my pussy. He was *huge,* and I huffed out a laugh that turned into a moan, not quite believing I could take him inside me.

When I reached down to play with my clit, Eldich's eyes snapped open as he felt my hand between us. "Yes…" he hissed out, and I quickly brought myself to orgasm, and my legs shuddered as I came again around his cock. Eldich's thrusts became sporadic, and his body jerked as he came inside me. I cried out at the sensation of his cum filling me.

He tried to pull out, but I wrapped my legs around his body and yanked him back to me, moaning as his still-hard cock sunk into me again. "No," I muttered as I rubbed his back. "Stay inside me."

Eldich chuckled softly, lowered himself onto his forearms, and rested his face against my neck. The heavy rush of his warm breaths shifted against my skin, and I squirmed at the sensation as we both came down from our highs.

"My mate..." he muttered against my skin. I sighed and wrapped my arms around him, not wanting to let him go.

"It's over, isn't it?" I whispered. I hated how tears immediately stung the back of my eyes, and I blinked them away. Eldich tried to shift, but I gripped him harder. I needed to feel him around me, over me, and in me. I needed him everywhere.

"It's over. You're safe. I'll protect you."

"And we can be happy here?"

"I'll give you everything you need and more." The growl in his chest started again, and I smiled even as I felt my throat constricting as I fought the urge not to cry. There was something in the back of my mind telling me this was too good to be true, that this was the same as when Misha escaped, only to be taken again. The entire thing was a setup and one day, the Ghaal would simply appear again and take Eldich away from me, and I'd be doomed to the life they'd brought me here for.

Eldich hummed against my skin and planted delicate kisses against my neck and cheek as I turned my face against him. "I'm sorry," I whispered, hating how the emotion sprung into my voice. "I just... need you."

"You've been through so much," Eldich said, and

I finally relinquished my hold on him just enough for him to lean back and look at me. He ran a thumb over my cheek and swiped away the tear that had escaped. "But you have me, and I'm not going anywhere."

He shifted again, and the movement caused his cock to move inside me. I moaned, and Eldich's eyebrows rose before a grin crept across his face. I couldn't help but smile back at him and took a moment to take in the lines of his face. Although his skin color and some of his more prominent physical features had changed, he was still Eldich in his eyes and face. I didn't see a Ghaal when I looked at him as he feared.

I saw only Eldich.

My mate.

I smirked at the term—calling him *my mate* instead of my *boyfriend* seemed strange. But also, strangely right.

"I only need you," I said, and Eldich responded by shifting his hips forward and sinking his cock deeper into me. He was still hard, and I moaned at the sensation.

"I need to fuck you again, Amy," he groaned out the words and had already started a steady thrust in and out of my needy pussy.

"But... the others..."

"They can wait." I giggled as he dove back down, wrapped his arms under me, and pulled me against him as he inhaled deeply against my neck. My giggle turned into a moan as he thrust harder and faster. "I need you to come some more around my cock first."

CHAPTER
25

ELDICH

Too much had happened too quickly.

The day after I woke, we gathered outside Ilk's cave and sat on the flat rocks. There was a strange feeling in the air because we were relaxed, but no one felt like they *should* be relaxed. This sense of safety had come off the back of acts of brutality I hoped never to have to repeat. We'd left the bodies of the Ghaal where they lay in the colony and the lab for scavengers to pick clean. The few carnivorous species that were around were rarely seen, and while the females were small enough to be in danger from them, they wouldn't dare come close with us around.

Tori and Misha leaned against the wall's gentle incline near the cave's entrance, relishing in the warmth of the rocks. I'd noticed Tori had stuck close to Misha today, and I wondered if she'd been doing it the entire time I was unconscious. Sahcor had previously mentioned that Tori felt it was her fault Misha was taken in the first place, so she found it difficult to let go of the sense of responsibility for Misha's safety.

Especially in light of her pregnancy.

Consequently, this meant Sahcor and Virti were often seen together around their mates but were happy to exist in each other's company. Vitri had suggested no fewer than four times already today that Sahcor name their child after him, and the more irritated Sahcor became at the suggestion, the more Vitri seemed to enjoy it. I smirked as I watched them bicker, and my gaze slid back to Misha and Tori, who shared a grin and an eye roll.

Lanir was less trusting.

Despite the events of the past few weeks, he was still skittish and would run off with Samara in the evenings to find their own place to rest rather than sharing the space inside Ilk's cave. They returned each morning, and while Samara would be with her friends, he would spend the first part of the morning skirting around the area before he'd settle. He and I had a small conversation this morning when he came to ask if I was okay, and I was grateful for the steps he'd taken to try to become more a part of us as a community, but it wasn't easy for him.

Ryth seemed uncertain what to do with himself and threw occasional looks at Tegan. I'm certain she knew he was looking, but she'd stare determinedly away from him whenever he was close. They were the only two unmated in the group, and it must be difficult for Ryth. He'd never force Tegan, but he was definitely interested. I remembered the whispers they'd shared in the woods outside the Ghaal colony and how he'd calmed her when no one else could.

Maybe she'd come around.

"I think I'm just too tired to make a decision," Amy said as she traced invisible patterns with her finger on the rock where she sat. She lay on her stomach with her legs kicked up behind her, and I rested a palm on her lower back. I needed to touch her and keep touching her to remind myself this was real, and she was mine.

"We all know why you're tired," Tori teased. A round of chuckling followed Tori's comment, and I glanced at Amy to find her smiling, even though her cheeks were flushed.

Erica grinned before her smile slowly dropped as she seemed to sort through her thoughts. "I get what Amy means, though. I know we've got choices to make about where and how we're going to live, but I think we just need to spend some time recouping and relaxing. It's been... *a lot*. And there's no deadline, right?"

"Everyone is welcome to stay here for as long as you wish," Ilk said.

He turned as a growl started in Lanir's chest, and I looked up to see his lip lifted into a snarl, even as he avoided our eye contact. "Actually," Samara spoke up as she rubbed Lanir's arm. "I think we might go back to Lanir's place. Just for a few days, then we'll come back." She turned to Erica. "Is that okay?"

Erica smiled. "You don't need my permission. Go get some."

Tori barked out a laugh, and Samara smiled slyly. "I think we just need to be alone for a bit. We'll head off tomorrow. Okay?" Her question was directed at Lanir, and he looked down at her. The growling continued but changed in tone as he stared hard at her with an intensity in his gaze I'd seen most of the day. He was struggling to be in the group, and I was thankful he had a mate who understood him. Lanir would try his best for her, but he needed space. Samara smiled at him. "Okay," she said as if his silence was answer enough to have the matter settled. "But now that Eldich is back with us, I think we need to celebrate tonight."

"Celebrate how?" Tori leaned forward.

Samara shrugged. "A party of some sort. Get lots of food. We can dance and sing."

Tori laughed before her lip twisted as she thought. "Pity there's no alcohol. Then we could make it a real party. Although…" she tapped her chin thoughtfully, "… there's always the rubaee plant to make us feel drunk."

"*No,*" Vitri snarled out, and Tori laughed. Vitri's eyes flashed dangerously as he stared her down where she sat, and his shadow covered her. Tori didn't even blink and simply stayed, grinning up at him before she started blinking at him rapidly and cupped her hands under her chin. Vitri's lip twitched after a beat, and his eyes narrowed as he smiled. "Careful, my mate," he teased in a whisper.

"The pilaee fruits ferment if left on the ground," Ryth said, and when Vitri stared at him, he shrugged. "Makes you feel a bit dizzy and happy. It's fun."

Tegan chuckled quietly, and Ryth threw her a smile she promptly looked away from.

Tori stared at him. "The *what* plants?"

"Pilaee," Vitri repeated as he drew a shape in the air with his fingers. "They're about this size with a deep green scale-like looking skin."

"You brought me some of those when we met," Tori piped up before she threw him a sly look. "You dog, were you trying to get me drunk to have your wicked way with me?"

Vitri swooped down, and his vines wrapped around her torso as he picked her up and crushed her body against his. "I don't need you drunk for that."

She laughed, even as she squirmed out of his hold before she turned to Ryth. "Are there any of those plants near here?"

He lifted a shoulder. "Might be around the other side of the mountain. I can go check and be back by tonight?"

"Yes, please," Erica said.

"Are they safe, Ryth?" Ilk asked.

"Never gave me a problem, and Tori said she's eaten them before." He waved a hand at her, and she nodded at Ilk. Ilk grumbled but said nothing else.

"But are they *safe*…" Amy placed a hand over her stomach as her brows pulled together, still battling conflicting emotions over the unknown. "For um… Misha and her baby?"

"Pilaee will not harm her baby."

"Even fermented?"

"Even fermented. Although…" he glanced at Misha and threw a grin at Sahcor. "Perhaps when she's breastfeeding, I wouldn't suggest it."

Ryth glanced at Tegan as though waiting for her to laugh again, but she said nothing, and after a pause, he slapped Ilk on his shoulder before he took off at a run.

"Let's start gathering some food. This is going to be fun!" Erica clapped her hands together.

I stood to help but stopped when the blood rushed to my head, and pops of light moved in front of my eyes. I held a palm to my forehead as it cleared. It only took a few seconds, and I took a deep breath. When I opened my eyes, Amy was immediately at my side. "Are you okay?"

"I'm fine. Just got a bit dizzy."

Her lips were pressed together in a line, and she clung to my arm as she looked up at me. "Maybe you should get some more rest."

I grunted. "I've rested enough. I can hunt with my brothers."

Before I took a step, Ilk was in front of me and shoved an armful of water bags against my chest. "Fill these. No hunting for you yet. I saw how you swayed when you stood."

"I'm fine," I grumbled.

"He's right, Eldich." Amy curled her fingers around the inside of my elbow and rubbed my arm with her other hand. "You should take it easy. I'll go with you to fill up the water bags." She tugged on my arm, and I bent to allow her to whisper in my ear. "Erica showed me the hot springs around the corner. We could bathe together." My cock jerked under my loin cloth at her words, and Amy giggled.

Thankfully, Ilk wasn't listening, and if he were, he didn't show it. He sighed heavily even as he smiled at me. "It's good to have you back with us." He turned to watch Erica as she excitedly chatted to Tori and Misha about the pilaee fruit. "I have a feeling we're going to need lots of extra water."

We'd built a large fire outside, cooked the meat, and laid out a selection of fruits. Everyone was eating, chatting, and drinking. Amy seemed genuinely happy, and I watched her interact with the other females from across the fire. I couldn't help but admire her body, and from the looks she threw me, I doubted she minded.

Amy would smile at me, and all the noise around us would melt away.

I couldn't wait to fuck her again.

Ryth had successfully found some fermented pilaee fruit and was busy watering the juice down at Ilk's insistence. Once the fruit was broken open, they were almost liquid inside, and the girls gathered around, excited to try the new treat, as he shook the mixed water bags up.

Ryth pressed the bag and released some liquid into his mouth before he smacked his lips. "That should do it." He found Tegan with his eyes as the females stood around him and reached out to her, holding the bag. "Would you like some?"

Tegan tensed as silence dropped over us. It was hard *not* to watch. I wanted Ryth to know the pleasure of having a mate, and I wanted Tegan to feel as safe and happy as Amy did. Tegan's face flushed an angry pink when she realized everyone was watching her for a reaction. She stared at the bag offered to her as if unsure what to do. Tori stepped forward and took the bag from Ryth, breaking the spell. He frowned at her, but she ignored him and turned to Tegan.

"Bottoms up," Tori announced, taking a swig before handing the bag to Tegan.

Tegan offered a small smile and shared a brief moment of eye contact with Tori before she, too, drank.

The bag was passed around between them while Ryth grabbed a whole fruit, broke it over his mouth, and drank the fermented liquid straight from the inside.

"It tastes like cheese," Erica said as she wiped her mouth with the back of her hand.

"That's *exactly* what I thought. Like a sweet cheese." Tori took a swig before she barked out a loud laugh. "*Whoa.* That's going to go *straight* to my head."

Misha sniffed it but declined to have any. However, Sahcor took a drink and squeezed it directly into his mouth as he stood behind Misha with his hands cupped over her belly. "I'm not sure it'll work on us as quickly as it does you," he said, smiling as Tori giggled.

Ryth broke another one of the fruits and squeezed it into his mouth, his pupils already dilated and a wide grin on his face. "We just need to have it undiluted." But when he offered a fruit to Sahcor with a smirk, Sahcor held his hand up and shook his head. Ryth handed them out to the rest of us, Lanir declining with a snarl and Ilk sipping it slowly. Ryth winked at me as he dropped the fruit into my hand. "It'll make you feel good," he said with a smirk. He nodded at Amy as we watched her help herself to the drink after Tegan. "You two can relax together."

"We've *been* relaxing," I huffed out.

Ryth's smile was gentle as he spoke lowly to me. "I know that. I'm just saying she's been through a lot, she and Tegan, they need to let go of the memories and have fun."

My brows furrowed as I closed my fingers around the fruit but thanked him under my breath as he moved on. I appreciated his concern, but Amy was *my* mate, and I would look out for her. I wondered what Ryth had gotten up to while we were separated. The forest he'd lived in was more densely populated with plants because of the river system, but none of the rest of us had sought out any mind-altering substances.

Amy *was* relaxed. I was sure of it. But she wouldn't be able to *let go* of the memories so quickly. They would stay inside her for a long time, perhaps forever, and I would do whatever she needed to help her feel better.

Amy stood with the other girls in a small circle. They sipped the drink and giggled amongst themselves as they handed the bag between them. I watched the light from the fire create flickers of shadows over her skin. Her legs and ass were hidden from me by the pants she wore, and I lifted my lip into a snarl. My cock jumped with interest every time I watched her, and all I wanted to do was keep her in the cave with me and fuck her over and over again. I wanted to taste her cunt on my lips and tongue before I kissed her while she moaned. I wanted to give her *all* the pleasure.

But Ryth was right. She needed this with her friends.

Amy was my mate—happy, healthy, and safe. I never wanted her to be any other way.

"Pity there's no music," Amy said as they finished the first bag between them. Ryth had mixed up several, and as I burst the fruit into my mouth and swallowed the liquid, I hoped he had watered it down enough for them. My head immediately spun, and I closed my eyes and waited for it to ease into a dull sense of relaxation. I blinked through the sensation, smiled, and tilted my head as Tori tutted, grabbed Amy's hands, and pulled her nearer the fire.

"Then we make our own music!"

Tori started singing, and after a few lines, Erica laughed and joined in. Soon, the girls were jumping around and singing together. When Amy stumbled slightly, I jumped to my feet, only for Samara to steady her as they giggled together. The song was strange, telling a story about a boy talking to a girl, but then she turned him down. I lost track of the story between the giggling and the screaming.

Was this purely the reaction of the pilaee fruit?

Or was this how humans celebrated?

My expression softened as I watched them. Perhaps it was only strange to me because I had never celebrated anything. I glanced at my brothers to find them watching the girls with equal looks of bemusement and confusion.

What have we had to celebrate previously? *Nothing.*

But now we did...

Safety.

Freedom.

A future with our mates.

Smiling, I moved to sit back down, but my standing had drawn the girls' attention to me, and Amy ran over, grabbed my hands, and pulled me into the center of their circle. I stood still, not wanting to move, while the girls jumped around me, kicking and moving their bodies to a beat I couldn't hear and didn't seem to match the singing. Vitri laughed as I stood awkwardly, and when Amy grabbed my hands and started waving my arms around, he clapped and joined in with the dancing. He tried to sing along with words he didn't know and made them up when he wasn't sure until Tori shoved him in the chest, laughing. He grabbed her arms and tugged her so she stumbled against him and kissed her hard.

The song ended, and the girls came and sat around the fire with us, still chatting and shrieking with laughter. I followed as Amy dragged me to sit, and the growl started deep in my chest when she sat on my lap, throwing an arm around my shoulder. I immediately buried my face against the crook of her neck, inhaled deeply, and hummed when she squirmed and giggled. Erica and Tori cooed at Ryth as he offered them another bag of the fruit drink, and they held their hands out eagerly. Tegan stood back slightly and waited for Erica and Tori to come to her.

"I haven't heard that song in forever," Samara said as she sat on Lanir's lap. He tucked his arms around her stomach and pressed his face against her hair, content to close his eyes and not talk.

"Definitely a pre-teen anthem," Erica said.

"What was the song?" Sahcor asked as if knowing the name would make any difference to us.

" "Best Song Ever" by One Direction," Amy answered before taking another drink.

"That was the best song ever made on your planet?" Sahcor asked, trying and failing to keep the judgment out of his tone.

Misha laughed. "It's just the name of the song."

Sahcor didn't understand, and I didn't either, but I didn't ask anything further.

"Although," Amy continued as she leaned her head against mine. "It wasn't a pre-teen or even a teenage anthem for me. I was twenty-four when that song came out."

"Whaaa...oooh..." Tori raised her finger then dropped it. "I forgot you were an Amy-sicle for a while."

Amy chuckled. "It's okay." She turned to me after she handed the drink bag to Tegan. "Can I ask you a question?"

"Of course," I said, although I couldn't help the creeping feeling of concern crawling up the back of my neck. Amy's eyes were slightly glazed over, and her cheeks flushed. She was giggling more than usual, and while the girls seemed to be having fun, the effect of the fermented pilaee fruit was strange. My head was spinning slightly, but unlike Amy, I didn't want to sing and jump around. I simply wanted to take her back to the cave and fuck her all night. But I wanted to do that anyway. I glanced over to Ilk and Erica to find them kissing passionately. Erica had her palm placed on his chest and her other hand around the back of his neck. Despite the size difference between them, she seemed to be the initiator. I smirked—*humans are strange.*

Perhaps I'd need to find another place to take Amy to be alone.

"What's the name of this planet?" Amy blurted out.

The other girls stared at me too. Even Erica pulled away from Ilk as if I held all the secret information they desired. I searched my mind, but there was no translation into their language for the name.

So, I said it in our language. "Quittiseeflomshe."

"Um… gesundheit?" Tori said, and Tegan snorted with laughter.

"Can you repeat that?" Amy asked.

Before I could answer, Erica laughed. "Sounded like *skittish flimsy.*"

"Flimsy, flamsy."

"Flamsy pants."

"Skittish pajama llama pants."

There was a round of laughter from the girls after this rapid exchange between them, and I glanced at my brothers, who seemed equally as confused as me.

With a smile, Misha handed me the drink bag without taking any herself after it was handed to her by Ryth, and I took it, taking a large gulp.

Maybe the girls would make more sense if I drank more with them.

CHAPTER 26

AMY

We sang a bit more, and we drank a *lot* more.

Our makeshift party turned out to be the best party I'd ever attended. It was simple and small, but it was everything I needed and more. I couldn't have imagined even a week ago that this was where I'd be, and while there were a lot of things I'd miss about Earth, I could actually see a future here.

A life with my mate, a family, friends—health and happiness.

But I would grieve for the family I had at home and all the things I would miss.

Before the sad thoughts I didn't want to focus on

right now took hold, I pulled myself away from a conversation with the girls and dropped myself back onto Eldich's lap. His arms immediately came around me and held me close, and I sighed as I smiled and leaned my head against his.

"Hello, my mate," I said with a smirk.

Eldich grinned. "Hello. Are you having fun?"

"Definitely. I feel great." I rubbed my head. "I think the buzz is starting to wear off a bit now."

"Would you like some more to drink?"

I laughed. "No thanks, I think I'm good." When I pulled back so I could look into his eyes, I couldn't keep the smile from my face. He looked… happy, and it warmed my heart. I stumbled over my next breath when I was assaulted with the memory of his dying body convulsing on the ground, and when he frowned at my reaction, I cleared my throat. "How are you feeling? You had some to drink too."

"I did. It didn't make me crazy, though."

My brows pulled together. "Why would it make you crazy?"

Eldich gestured to the girls who were currently trying to teach Ilk a playground clapping game. Ilk's movements were sluggish as he tried to keep up with the rhyme and simultaneously hold back on his strength. It certainly didn't help when Tori joined in and made the two-way game a three-way and utterly confused poor Ilk, much to Vitri's joy. I rolled back against Eldich as I laughed. "We're not *crazy.* We're just having fun."

Eldich's chuckle was a deep rumble in his chest as I settled against him again. "Well, I didn't feel the urge to dance and sing."

"What did you feel the urge to do?"

His hips jolted under me, and I felt the hard line of his cock through our layers of clothes. "Oh…" My pussy throbbed at the thought of how good his cock had felt inside me and how hard he'd made me come. The noise from the party died away as I focused on the feeling of Eldich's body under mine—his arms around me, the heat of his breath against my neck, and the hard lines of his arms and chest.

"I need you, Amy." The words were a rumble, and I whimpered as I ground myself against his cock. When we were at the springs earlier, I'd given him a hurried hand-job after a heated make-out session. Eldich was still trembling after his orgasm when Tegan came around the corner, apparently looking for me. She'd cried out and turned away when she realized we were naked in the spring, and I felt conflicting feelings of guilt and annoyance at our sexy time being interrupted.

Tegan hadn't brought it up since, so neither did I.

"Where can we go?" I asked as I eyed Erica and Ilk. She'd been pawing at him for the past hour or so, and he was no longer able to hide his erection.

They'd go to his cave soon.

"Come."

Eldich stood and steadied me as I slid off his lap. Sahcor and Ryth glanced up as we stood and simply smirked but said nothing as Eldich placed a hand on my lower back and ushered me away from the fire. We walked over the rocks as they flattened out—they still held a touch of warmth from the daylight sun. It wasn't late enough for the winds to start just yet, but I didn't want to be caught in them.

The rocks turned into soft grasses, and Eldich guided me through them for a while before he stopped. When I turned, I could see the glow of the fire in the distance and barely heard a hum of conversation and laughter.

"Eldich—"

But his mouth was on mine, swallowing whatever I was going to say—*what was it? Can't have been that important if I can't remember with his tongue distracting me. Probably wondering out loud if they'd be able to hear us.* But I found I didn't care. This wasn't home, and an entirely new set of rules needed to be developed. We'd figure it out together another day, but if we *were* going to be living in close quarters, chances are we'd see each other naked or hear each other having sex.

I didn't particularly care, but I'm not sure all the girls would feel the same.

Eldich's tongue was working circles around

mine, and I moaned at the taste of him and the hint of the lingering fruity flavor. With one hand on the back of my head, he used the other to tug at my pants, and I helped him before I shimmed out of them and kicked them to the side. We broke apart long enough for me to pull my tunic over my head before he was kissing me again.

We moved to our knees without breaking the kiss, and I pulled the knot at the side of his loin cloth undone and grabbed his hard cock, taking a moment to work my fingers on the lines of him. Eldich sucked in a breath at my ministrations, groaned into my mouth, pulled away from the kiss, and inhaled in a lungful of air. "Lie down," I said, still almost breathless from the kiss and the anticipation.

He looked like he was about to argue, his eyes tracing the lines of my body before coming to rest on my face. He did as I asked, laid down in the grass, and I crawled over him before straddling him. When I shifted my hips, the hard length of his cock rubbed against my clit, and I moaned at the sensation. When Eldich reached for me, I grabbed his hands and guided him to tuck them under his head.

His eyelids were hooded as he watched me, and I smiled. The desire in his expression was clear in the moonlight, and as I sat atop him, I felt beautiful and powerful.

Wanted.

Unable to wait any longer, I adjusted myself onto my knees so I could position the head of his cock at my pussy, already wet and dripping for him. His mouth opened, jaw slacked, and his eyes closed as I lowered myself onto him before his arms shot out to grip my thighs.

"Oh my God, Eldich, you feel so good…"

"Your cunt feels amazing, my mate…" he muttered.

His hands remained gripped on my thighs as I lowered myself fully onto him, taking my time and savoring every inch as he stretched me open for him. When my hips were flush with his, I stilled, and my body shuddered with the sensation overload. The winds had started to pick up, and Eldich yanked the strip of fabric I had over my breasts down and watched my nipples harden in the cool air.

My legs trembled. Everything about Eldich turned me on, and I gasped with pleasure as his large hands encompassed my breasts and squeezed gently. The *idea* of sex with him was enough to get me wet, so by the time he was inside me, I was already pulsing the edge of orgasm.

And to top that we were *free.*

Slowly, I lifted myself before dropping hard back down onto him, causing his cock to go just that little bit deeper when I didn't think it could. I cried out, arched my back, and threw my head back as I rode him. Eldich groaned, and I looked down at him. He was still gazing up at me as if he couldn't get enough of me.

With a smile, I placed my palms on his chest and tilted forward. Eldich kept his hands on my breasts, and I leaned into his touch before I started thrusting my hips harder, riding his cock. I wanted every inch of him and to feel him pulse inside me as I gripped him. I needed to feel his skin and the lines of his chest under my fingers and the grip of his hands on my thighs. This was the freedom he had promised me, the life together he told me about. The stretch of him inside me made me tremble, and I paused in my thrusting to drop down and feel him fill me up completely.

Eldich wanted me.

He *loved* me.

And I loved him back.

Eldich's groans increased in volume, and I giggled, knowing they could almost definitely hear him back by the fire. *Let them hear. He's my mate, and he is being pleasured,* I thought with a smirk.

My giggle brought Eldich's gaze to my face, his pupils blown wide and a snarl on his lips. He shifted his hands to my hips and gripped harder to still my movements before he guided me to rise to my knees until just the head of his cock was inside me.

I tried to sink back down on him, desperate for the fullness he had taken from me. I clenched, the head of his cock promising pleasure. But he held me still, and when I moaned in frustration and raised a questioning eyebrow, he simply smirked.

Without warning, he thrust up into me hard and didn't stop.

He held me in place and pounded into me from below until my pussy clenched on him, and I cried out, my scream of pleasure ending in a jolted laugh as I came.

"Oh my God, *Eldich.*" He kept going, and I fell forward and planted my palms on his chest as he continued to thrust up into me. Eldich's forehead was covered in a thin sheen of sweat, and the growl in his chest thundered under my fingertips. He held me still as he used my pussy to draw himself closer to release, and every drag of his cock across my G-spot was an exquisite pleasure. I'd feel empty without him, I knew it, and would take the overstimulation of him fucking me through the aftershocks of my orgasm any day. I wanted to wake up with his cock sinking into me and his lips on my neck. I wanted his fingers and tongue in me as he made those delectable sounds like I was the most delicious thing he'd ever tasted. I closed my eyes as I thought of wrapping my lips around the head of his cock while he slept and having him wake with a pleasured groan before he grabbed my hair and thrust into my mouth.

And I could have all those things with him, and

we had all the time to explore each other.

With a roar, Eldich came, and he pulled me down until his cock sunk deep inside me. The warm rush of his cum painting my walls made me tremble with pleasure.

"Fuck," I muttered as I collapsed onto his chest. Eldich's arms came around my body and held me close against him. "Fuck," I repeated with a laugh.

"Again?" Eldich grumbled, and I laughed once more, even as my pussy clenched around his cock at the thought. He was still hard, and I wanted him to stay inside me.

I wanted more.

I wanted it *all.*

"You make me feel so good, Eldich," I muttered as I sighed and placed my forehead against his. "And I don't just mean the sex." His eyes snapped open, and I was dazzled by the bright green of his irises in the moonlight as he stared at me. "Would it be too much to tell you I love you?"

He shook his head slowly, never breaking eye contact with me. "I thought you already knew I loved you."

I smiled before I pressed my lips against his. Eldich groaned and parted his lips, inviting my tongue into his mouth to play with his. His hips began to rock against mine, and his cock swelled impossibly harder inside me as I moaned into his mouth.

"Again?" he whispered.

"Yes, again." I lifted and dropped my hips to match his movements, slowly dragging his cock in and out of me, making my legs shake with pleasure. He always had me on the edge of coming without even trying, and I clamped my thighs around his hips. "And again, and again..." I muttered as I pressed kisses to his neck and shoulder. Eldich growled and grabbed me, rolling us over until I was underneath him. The slick drag of his cock inside me was ecstasy, and I moaned in delight as he fucked me with a steady rhythm, torn somewhere between taking his time and fucking me hard until we were both limp with pleasure.

Outside of the feel of Eldich's body, my mind was blank. There was a world of things I needed to consider—where we would live being the main one.

Would we stay together as a group?

Would the brothers want that?

I knew next to nothing about their young—did Eldich know how to raise a baby? Did I? How would it be different from my niece? What would the baby look like? Would we be better as a group because we could help each other? Misha was already pregnant.

Eldich hummed against me when he noticed I'd stilled and grabbed my chin until I looked into his eyes. He jolted his hips against me, and I released a sharp cry of pleasure as he filled me. "What are you thinking, my mate?" He rumbled, and I sighed even as my lips curled into an uncertain smile.

"Where do we go from here?"

"Anywhere we want," he said, and we both groaned as he began a deep, slow thrust into me. "Anywhere we want."

THE END

Continue with…
Freer – Elements of Abduction Book 6
for
Tegan and Ryth's story

The human women are free, but Tegan feels suffocated under the expectation of becoming Ryth's mate.
When something changes and threatens to tear apart the fragile grasp Tegan has on herself, perhaps even Ryth's love can't save her.

ACKNOWLEDGMENTS

Book Five!

That means there's only one more book in this series—stay tuned for *Freer,* Tegan and Ryth's story.

This section will be short this time, I promise. But I can't say the same for the next book because I tend to get emotional and might ramble for a bit, and I'll apologize to no one for that.

This series has been a joy to write, and I still shake my head to think it started with such a small spark of an idea—what if there were aliens who adapted to their environments and, therefore, looked like the elements? Water, earth, fire… and it grew from there. Ilk was, of course, the first one to stroll into my mind—or lumber in—looking like he was made of stone with a lopsided grin. And from there, it simply *flowed.*

There are some difficult topics covered in these books, and the heroines have gone through some unpleasant things. But I hope the general feel of family, community, and love was enough to keep this series a mostly light and enjoyable read.

Dare I ask who's your favorite Synth?
It's Vitri, isn't it?
Hmm… maybe Lanir. I'm a sucker for a big guy who needs a hug.

I'm looking forward to bringing you Book Six.

And thank you for reading!

CONNECT WITH ME ONLINE

ANGELS AND FIRE BOOKS

Find our exciting stories at:

www.angelsandfirebooks.com.au

READER GROUP

Want access to fun, prizes and sneak peeks?
Join my Facebook Reader Group.
https://www.facebook.com/groups/588038442170571

NEWSLETTER

Sign up for my Newsletter.
https://www.subscribepagye.com/angelsandfirebooks

BOOKBUB

https://www.bookbub.com/authors/stefanie-dawn

GOODREADS

Add my books to your TBR list
on my Goodreads profile.
https://www.goodreads.com/author/
show/21761217.Stefanie_Dawn

AMAZON

https://www.amazon.com/author/stefaniedawn

WEBSITE

http://www.angelsandfirebooks.com.au/

INSTAGRAM

https://www.instagram.com/angelsandfirebooks

EMAIL

info@angelsandfirebooks.com.au

FACEBOOK

https://www.facebook.com/stefaniedawnwriter

ABOUT THE AUTHOR

Stefanie Dawn has been a writer and creative soul all her life **and** strives to give her readers stories they can escape into as they become absorbed in the worlds created.

When she isn't writing, Stefanie might be painting, reading, or watching movies. She loves the process of producing films as another form of storytelling. There's also a good chance she'll be baking some delicious treats—pretending she won't later regret consuming them—or simply enjoying a cocktail with friends.

Stefanie Dawn lives in South Australia with her ever-supportive partner and a lovable gang of rescue cats.

You can stay up to date with
Stefanie and her books at:
www.angelsandfirebooks.com.au